N GRAY

Chasing Evil

VINCI
BOOKS

Vinci Books

vinci-books.com

Published by Vinci Books Ltd in 2025

1

Copyright © Maya Daniels 2024

The publisher and the author have made every effort to obtain permissions for any third party material used in this book and to comply with copyright law. Any queries in this respect should be brought to the attention of the publisher and any omissions will be corrected in future editions.
A CIP catalogue record for this book is available from the British Library.
Paperback ISBN: 9781036706630

Chapter One

BROOKLYN

At some point in everyone's life, a person comes to realize that they do believe in fairy tales. The reason for this realization is simple: everyone lies.

And we lie the best to ourselves.

The exact same thing I was currently doing in hopes to justify everything that happened from the moment Veronica was killed until I almost killed Alice in my bloodlust. Every day, every mistake I made flickered and spun behind my mind's eye, taunting me to a point of madness.

I had good intentions for all of it from day one, even when I sought revenge. The gods know I did. We meant well with all our actions, which led us to a point of no return. In our righteousness, we slowly became the monsters we were hunting. A head-spin rocked my body sideways, and the world around me tilted on its axis for a scary second.

I almost killed Alice.

Dominic almost killed Alice by placing her in my path when I couldn't tell a friend from a foe.

All I knew was blood.

I still remembered the gnawing hunger for her blood clawing at the back of my throat.

I remembered the taste too and wished I could die a thousand deaths because saliva immediately pooled in my mouth from the memory.

A tremor zipped from my tailbone to the base of my skull, and I shivered slightly, eyes jumping guiltily from the twisted fingers in my lap to the pale face of my friend, which looked too small nestled in the huge pillows Samir insisted she rest upon. Her sluggish heartbeat spit and stuttered in her chest like the timeworn van her late father left her in case alien monsters attacked the human race.

No outer space creatures came, but he was probably turning in his grave from the fact that she chauffeured monsters around in that rusted can. Behemoths that were a danger to her no matter which way you looked at it. There were no doubts left about what we were anymore.

We were monsters that would've and still could cost her, her life.

In this entire nightmare, she was the only one with the heart in the right place—the only innocent one.

She should've been somewhere safe. I should've made sure of it. All the many would'ves and should'ves circled like vultures through my mind, tormenting me without a pause. I'd go insane if this continued. And we all knew where that led. Everyone I cared about had a front row seat to that one.

"You can't keep doing this to yourself." As if reading my mind, Samir muttered under his breath from his spot against the wall so that only I could hear him. He did it without opening his eyes or lowering his face that he had tilted upward at the high ceiling. "You are coherent enough to be a thorn in the side to all of us but not recovered as much as you should be if the Syndicate comes knocking. You are not doing any favors for any of us if you are weak."

He'd been a permanent fixture next to the bed after he placed Alice on it, growling like a wild beast at anyone who suggested he move. On the opposite side of the ancient Atua, the wolf was stretched out on the floor, his snout propped on his folded front paws with one eye open and the upper lip permanently curled over razor sharp teeth in a snarl as a warning. Everything was as it should be in order to give me that peace of mind that no harm would come to my friend. Yet, guilt gnawed a hole in my stomach, warning me that the threat was here; I just couldn't see it. That if I even dared blink, Death would take her away from me forever the same way it took Veronica.

It took my breath away to realize you could love someone so much that the very feeling would be enough to fuel blinding hatred toward everyone and everything around you that wanted to hurt them. That love was strong enough to make you hate yourself even if you placed them, intentionally or not, in harm's way.

Instead of sharing my epiphany, I pushed it away. Samir needed a lecture on hypocrisy for sharing his wisdom uninvited. "The same way you are not doing us any favors by not sleeping or feeding, you mean? There is no difference if I sit here or in the bedroom three doors down. I'm recovering right in front of you as we speak." Tiredly, I rubbed a hand over my face and grimaced when I looked down at my palm. Crusted blood and dirt flaked off of my skin and floated all over my pants, identifying me as a liar. "You could make yourself useful and bring me a wet washcloth though, if you don't mind." He answered my raised eyebrow with one of his own after he excruciatingly slowly lowered his head to make eye contact. "Or not," I amended bleakly.

His answering snort spoke volumes about my audacity to order him around, but things were different now. We were both different. He was no longer my master nor was I an obedient fool. Not that I'd ever been amenable and subservient. However, that never stopped him from sticking his nose where it didn't belong.

"You can't keep ignoring or avoiding him forever either." We both knew who he was referring to. Holding eye contact, Samir dared me to look away so he could call me a coward for trying my best to avoid the panther shifter. That privilege was afforded only to Alice, so I didn't dare move an eyelash as I stared back at him. Even when the corner of my eye became itchy, you'd think my body was doing things on purpose so that I would lose the staring match with the ancient pain in my butt.

"Since when did you become a country fair fortune teller giving unwanted relationship advice to poor souls?" The knowing glint in his dark eyes that saw way too much made me keep talking so I didn't scratch at my face. "I remember the times when you aspired to provoke fear from everyone around you, not eye rolling." And I proceeded to do just that. I rolled my eyes dismissively.

"I never took you for..." Samir started.

"Don't say it." All unwanted sensations forgotten, I hissed through clenched teeth, my fingernails digging into the palms of my fisted hands. A piece of hair escaped my ponytail, and the red strand licked the side of my face like a flickering flame, just enough to anger me more. I yanked it back behind my ear. "I have never been, nor would I ever be, a coward!"

"Very well." With a mocking smirk, he inclined his head

regally at me and narrowed his gaze. "You have always been logical with both feet rooted to the ground. There is nothing wishy washy in the Brooklyn I know. Everything Dominic did was because he loves you. You know this to be true. He was ready to rip the worlds apart to get you back. You cannot fault him for trying to do even the impossible to save his mate. Realms have been destroyed by males doing what is necessary to protect their mates and keep them safe."

"You think I judge my mate too harshly for his actions? I judge myself more for everything I did, and tainted blood is not a passable excuse for being a remorseless, unrepentant killer." The legs of the chair screeched loudly as they scraped over the wooden floors when I jumped to my feet, fists balled at my sides so I didn't wrap my hands around Samir's neck. "Who died and made him God so that he could decide who lives and who dies? Who?" Tears burned at the back of my eyes and a fist was lodged in my throat, making my voice crack. "We have no right to decide anyone's fate. None of us do. We are monsters!" A treacherous tear rolled over my cheekbone and stubbornly dangled on my jawline long enough for the older male to be able to track it with his eyes.

"Easy now, child." Both hands lifted to the sides, palms facing me in a placating motion, as he pushed off the wall and took a step toward me. "It will take a few more days for the tainted blood to fully release its hold. Rage is still fast to overpower logic. Take a deep breath and stay calm."

All I saw was red while his voice was muted and too far away for me to hear without straining. Somewhere in the back of my mind, I was aware that something was wrong, but I couldn't get a grip on my emotions to save my life. Like slippery silk, they trickled between my fingers to escape my hold.

"Men." The barely audible sound of Alice's voice doused all of my anger with the strength of a bucket of iced cold water, yanking me back to the present with a slingshot, like nothing ever would've been able to. Both Samir and I turned sharply to stare wide-eyed at the human eyeing us dazedly from the mountain of pillows. "A sure way to meet your maker before it's your time to go is to tell a pissed off woman to calm down. It goes as well as trying to pet a cat after keeping her tied in a bag for a couple of days. No offense to Dominic." My friend attempted to make a joke with a forced smile for my benefit, and my heart clenched painfully in my chest at the gammy grimace that twisted her features. "No one told the poor dude that, huh?"

My mouth opened and closed a few times, but my throat was dry, and no sound came out. All of us, including the wolf who raised his head when Alice spoke, stood frozen in disbelief. Her face swam as my eyes filled with tears and traveled unchecked when they trickled down my face. All that I managed was an embarrassing croak before I rushed the bed and collapsed on it with heart wrenching sobs that were ripped from the very center of my being.

"You." With shaking fingers, I latched on to her cold hand. It felt like it was the only thing keeping me from exploding into a million pieces. "Are…awake."

"Oh, Brooklyn." She murmured and tried to squeeze my hand. I only knew this because her fingers twitched and that was all the strength she had. I tightened my hold on her instead, mindful not to break her bones.

"I am, so, so, sorry, Alice!" Sobs kept wracking my hunched shoulders. "This is all my fault. All of it. But I will make it right. I promise you I'll make it right."

"The Syndicate did this, not you." Her voice broke, and she started coughing weakly. Samir was there in an instant, shoving me out of his way and holding her up so he could press a glass of water with a straw to her lips. "None of us…did anything…wrong."

"Shhhh, don't talk." He cooed at Alice like he was hushing a newborn. "Talking can wait for when you are stronger."

He glanced at me quickly to make sure I was paying attention. "She has times where she wakes up for a minute or two, but it costs her dearly." After brushing a strand of hair from her sweaty forehead, he pressed the glass more insistently to her dry, cracked lips. "Sip now, *Esme.*"

I froze, as did he.

Well, well. What do you know.

The ancient Atua recovered quickly and continued his whispering encouragements for Alice to sip the water while I stared stunned at the back of his head. He used the ancient Persian word for beloved to address my friend. My first reaction was to snap his neck—immediately. The second reaction that rose within me had a more permanent consequence that was way too tempting, but I had to shake the urges away. I must've missed a lot of things while bloodlust was behind the wheel driving me all over Chicago.

There was a time and place for everything, I'd learned. So, when Samir glanced at me over his shoulder, his ancient eyes guarded, I gave him a sharp nod to tell him I planned on keeping my mouth shut and staying out of whatever was going on between him and my friend.

For now.

I could always kill him later.

That sounded like a delightful plan if I've ever heard one.

The future was looking brighter by the minute if you asked me.

Chapter Two

I left Samir to tend to Alice while I walked out into the hallway. I closed the door with a soft click before leaning my forehead against it and shutting my eyes. The cold wood of the door was a much-needed reprieve to my heated skin. A total opposite of other times when my body was a frozen popsicle waiting for spring thaw and I resembled a corpse. My internal temperature was really out of whack since I snapped out of my bloodlust. So I took a deep breath, allowing my shoulders to drop, not worried that anyone would see my weakness. The house was as silent as a tomb —so much so that the rhythm of my heart was echoing too loud in my ears.

I was tired.

Carrying a chip on my shoulder had become second nature, and I didn't notice the weight of it anymore. The guilt and responsibility of those around me, however, was a newly formed burden, which pressed so hard on my shoulders that it made it difficult to walk most days without doubling over. In the last few days or so I had a lot of time to think and reexamine my actions.

I was pretty sure anyone would agree when I said I acted rashly. A million excuses came to mind that could ease my culpability and justify everything. Be that as it may, I refused to use my rage and thirst for revenge as a crutch for placing everyone I cared about in danger. A slip up here and there in the name of a righteous indignation was one thing. But everyone suffering, or God forbid, dying, because I couldn't seem to get a grip on myself was a totally different story.

Enough was enough.

I stood there for hours it seemed, pressing my hands to my cheeks to cool them off and rolling my head all over the door while my mind raced, not wanting to miss the chance to taunt me with everything I'd done wrong. Lost in my thoughts, I didn't notice when the energy around me shifted, thickening the air and making it pregnant with tension. It spoke volumes about my current state and how much I needed to lie down so I could fully recover.

Not that I'd do it.

But it was telling.

"You are not feeling well?" Dominic asked but didn't approach me. It cost him dearly to keep his distance now that we'd opened Pandora's box by acknowledging the mate bond we so expertly avoided all this time.

"I'll be all right." My lips grazed the now warmed up wood of the door when I answered, keeping my eyes closed still so I didn't tempt myself to turn around and rush into his arms.

My whole being was tense, coiled like a rusted spring waiting to snap at the slightest brush of a breeze. There was no way in all hells that he didn't notice the slight tremor of my fisted hands or the coppery scent of my blood pooling in the small crescent cuts my nails left in my palms. Still, I stayed glued to the spot as if that would keep me away from the tsunami of emotions threatening to overwhelm me.

"Brooklyn, we can't keep doing this to each other." His voice came from much closer, although I didn't hear him move. Damn cats and their stealth. The hurt from my rejection was evident in the slight rasp of his tone and it took all the energy I had left not to visibly shiver. "You can be angry with me, hate me if that is what you want, but I don't and will not regret my actions. Ever."

My fist was lodged in my throat, closing it effectively up; and I swallowed thickly in hopes it would go down and I'd tell Dominic to leave me alone. Instead, my body began to quiver, and much to my embarrassment, my knees gave out.

That was all the signs he needed. He was there in an instant, scooping me up before I made contact with the floor. His male scent surrounded me from all sides, wrapping me tightly into a Dominic cocoon. My nose was full of him, my head was swimming from the fast pumping of blood my brain received while my heart jackhammered behind my ribcage with the strength of a tornado.

He was warm. Too warm under my clammy fingers that clung to any part of him I could reach like a lifeline. No matter how hard I wanted to push him away, scream at him that he almost killed Alice, my body had a mind of its own. I was acutely aware of every inch where he connected with me. The hard expanse of his muscled body molded to my smaller frame as he curled inward, as if he was trying to absorb me inside of him so that I could never get away. And I let him, curling firmly into his chest, my knees almost touching my chin.

Samir nagged that I couldn't avoid the shifter forever,

but this was the very reason why I'd been like a skittish mouse racing through the hallways of the enormous house, hoping I wouldn't run into him around every corner. I knew once he had his hands on me it would be game over.

Heat bloomed in my lower belly, and arching my back in his hold, I pressed my mouth onto his. A sharp intake of breath was the only sign that he never expected the situation to go in that direction, but he recovered quickly, and his warm wet tongue parted my lips with the desperation of a man dying from thirst faced with a glass of ice cold water.

I couldn't think, couldn't breathe, or even summon a drop of will to push him away. Surrendering to the force pulling us toward each other, I could only exist and feel. Twisting the longer strands of his hair between my fingers, I pulled him closer, chasing his tongue with mine while he explored the cavern of my mouth, leaving no space unturned.

My stomach dipped when he dropped my legs and spun me around so fast that I gasped for air before exhaling loudly when my chest was pressed hard to the door. For a split second, I wondered if Samir would open it to mock me for giving in to my baser needs; but then Dominic wrapped my ponytail around his hand and twisted my face around as much as it would allow before shoving his tongue in my mouth again. All thoughts about the ancient Atua fled my mind.

It was impossible to take a full breath the way I was pressed between the door and Dominic's body, his hard cock wedged between my butt cheeks pulsing in sync with his thrusting tongue. With one hand guiding my head with a firm hold on my hair, he snaked his other hand around my waist and excruciatingly slowly started gliding down my belly.

I gasped in his mouth when his fingers dipped inside the waistband of my pants, popping the buttons open one by one until the tips grazed the soft skin of my belly right above my panties. My ass pressed harder into his erection, encouraging him to hurry up and place his hand where I desperately needed it. There was a pulse between my legs painfully throbbing and begging for relief. But suddenly, the shifter was in no rush to save me from my misery. Oh no. Instead of plunging his fingers inside me, he started making tiny, gentle circles on my skin, driving me insane with need. No amount of wiggling or pressing against him could change his mind or even make him hurry it up. I thought I was losing my hold on reality when I heard a sound, but the vibration moving from his lips to mine told me I wasn't going crazy.

He chuckled.

In his right mind, he chuckled low and growly in my mouth, not pausing the kiss for a second as if my willingness to answer the call my body and the mate bond demanded was funny to him. The familiar burn of anger swirled in the center of my chest, and this time I pushed harder at his body crowding me, not to get closer but to get him off of me.

The arm around my waist tightened painfully, a warning from an alpha male that was attempting to solidify his dominance, but the feline shifter picked the wrong female for that. With a firmer shove, he finally got the message and uncoiled from around me but didn't step back, nor did he remove his mouth from mine. Instead of plundering it with his tongue, he peppered my lips with closed mouth kisses each time our noses connected, forcing me to blink.

"I'm not your enemy," he murmured between pecks,

and I stiffened. He paused kissing me long enough to search my gaze with his for a moment, but he repeated it again after not too long. "I am not your enemy, Brooklyn."

"Could've fooled me." Hating the way I sounded breathless and throaty, I shoved harder to get him to release me. "Get off of me."

"No." Still and unperturbed, he stared unblinkingly at me. "Talk to me."

"I have nothing to say. Now, get off of me." This time I did use my strength instead of the half-assed attempts I'd been giving him. "It's best to keep our distance for now. We need to figure out how to help Alice heal instead of wasting time on nonsense."

"This"—watching me with a raised eyebrow from a couple of steps away where I made him stumble back, he flicked a finger between us—"us, we are the nonsense?"

"She can die at any moment because of this." Mockingly, I flicked my own finger between us, imitating him. It caused a vein to jump on one side of his jaw and his eyes to narrow dangerously at me. "Us, as you like to say. I need to go."

My mouth opened to unleash the torrent of hurtful words that were flooding my brain at that moment but the clearing of a throat from further down the hallway put a stop to it. Later down the road, I would look back at this moment and be eternally grateful for the interruption; but as things were, I turned my glare on Rowen. The witch stood unnaturally still in the middle of the hall. You'd think he appeared there out of thin air.

A muted glow danced all over his tattoos, flickering like the tiny flames on dying embers from his forehead across his nose and down his chin only to disappear into the collar of his T-shirt. Green eyes—so pale it was almost impossible to see the color of the irises unless you had supernatural sight —saw way too much for my liking. They looked straight, not into my gaze, but into my soul. It was so unnerving, I instinctively took a step toward Dominic, which did not go unnoticed, much to my annoyance.

The witch made me apprehensive, to say the least.

"Can I help you?" I barked at him snidely and felt horrible the next second.

It was not his fault that all my nightmares were associated with witches and those vexatious sigils permanently marking his skin. If anything, he should've given me hope with his presence and willingness to help prove that not all of them were brainwashed puppets with no promise of redemption. That maybe, just maybe, my mother was not a villain waiting to strike from the shadows like a snake hiding in the grass. Alice's smiling face floated tauntingly in my mind's eye a second before it twisted into a horrified expression and blood gushed between her fingers wrapped around her neck.

"No," Rowen said softly and moved toward me, his robes brushing the floor delicately. If I didn't know any better, I would've thought he was floating. "But I do believe I can help you."

"I don't need your help." Snapping out of the daze the swirling robes put me in, I clenched my jaw. "And don't come anywhere near me." Stabbing a finger in his direction, I called on all the willpower I had left not to pounce on him, and rip open his jugular. Something felt off about the situation, but I couldn't put my finger on it. "Rowen, I mean it, I will kill you if you don't stop."

"You need my help, Brooklyn." Ignoring all the warnings and baring my fangs in his face, he kept gliding toward me. Dominic, on the other hand, stood there like a lump just mutely watching. "Allow me to bring you peace." The witch reached for my face, but instead of touching me, he pressed the open veins of his wrists to my lips.

Bitter fluid thick as tar filled my mouth, and I gagged, spitting it out as fast as I could while tears filled my eyes and trickled down my face. Just when I thought I had it all spat out, more poured in and Dominic pressed a hand over my lips, forcing me to swallow it down. It felt like liquid flames burned their way down to my belly, the pain was so intense I had no other option but to pass out.

Darkness claimed me but not before I saw Dominic's blanched face above mine. That only meant one thing. Something was wrong.

Something was horribly wrong.

Chapter Three

Reality came rushing in through increments a few minutes at a time. Some were calm and collected where I could hear familiar voices of people around me talking in hushed tones, others were from a fantasy movie with distorted faces of monsters, black blood pouring down my throat so bitter I prayed to whoever would listen to allow me to die so I didn't have to endure it anymore. Through it all, there was one constant. Well two if you count the guilt over Alice as a thing.

Dominic's hand held mine. Not helping when I begged him to kill me but not letting go when I felt like I would float away and disappear into nothingness either. Somewhere in the back of my mind a voice was persistent that I needed to wake up. But the moment I tried to open my eyes, searing pain would stab my retinas and I'd promptly pass out after a shrill scream.

"She should've been awake by now if you are telling the truth." A familiar voice growled as I struggled to place it. At first, I thought it was my tormentor and savior from the

16

nearby cage who refused to let me die in peace. But no. This voice was distinctly male, unlike the one reaching my ears from the dark shadows of the cages. Plus, I was on a soft, nicely scented mattress, and not on top of packed dirt soaked with my body fluids.

"Do something." That same deep voice grumbled and the hand holding mine tightened the hold.

"She's coming around." A second voice muttered from right above me. "It's taking longer than I expected but I also have no explanation why we found her collapsed in the hallway. She seemed okay when I saw her in passing this morning."

"Brooklyn?" Dominic cupped my face and turned it to the sound of his voice. "Can you hear me? Open your eyes, love. Look at me."

A memory filled me of his mouth on mine, his tongue swirling with my tongue, the feel of the slightly raspy texture sending a shiver through my body. Heat bloomed everywhere I remembered his hands touching and an embarrassing moan was ripped from my throat so guttural I felt my face burn in an instant.

"I'd say she's awake." Clearing his throat, the second male that I recognized now as Rowen the witch, couldn't hide his amusement. "I will go check on the human. The potions I brewed keep her barely alive and her situation can go sideways fast. Don't allow Brooklyn to get out of this bed until we are sure she won't collapse again. The last thing we need is the Syndicate getting their hands on her again. If you need me, you can find me there."

A soft click after a moment indicated that Rowen had left while I still gave everything I had to unglue my eyelids. It was as if some invisible power was holding them down and no amount of struggling helped. I was horrified that my heartbeat was still hammering loud enough to wake the dead while the shifter with his acute hearing was looming over me, his face close enough I could feel the heat of his skin from the nearness.

"It's okay." His deep voice reverberated in my chest, sending me on another hormone filled spin down the gutter. "Don't force it, Brooklyn. There is no danger. You can take your time—as long as you need." Callused fingers brushed a strand of hair from my face, the gesture too simple to be felt as intimately as I was feeling it.

I was losing my mind. There was no other explanation for my reaction to Dominic.

I mean the shifter was every female's wet dream, but I had always been able to hold tight control over my hormones and basic needs. Unlike most of my kind, I didn't trust anyone enough to allow them to share my vulnerable moments, be it sex, feeding, or the universe forbid, sleeping next to me. It must be the tainted blood and the prolonged process of healing as it was purged from my system that muddled my brain.

I convinced myself that it was true.

After a while, slowly, my eyes adapted to the light, and I managed to crack them open wide enough to make out Dominic's handsome face. Worry wedged two grooves between his eyebrows, and the five-o-clock shadow I was used to seeing was longer than I remember it. The dark strands of his hair were sticking out every which way, tousled over his forehead as if he'd been running his fingers through it; and the white t-shirt he wore was creased and crinkled, indicating he'd at least slept in it for one night. Disheveled as he was, he had no right to look so damn handsome or irresistible that my fingers were twitching from the need to touch him. Even the dark smudges under his eyes looked good, emphasizing the intense green color of his eyes.

"I've lost my mind." I blurted out, still unable to look away from him.

"Tell me something I don't know." One side of his full lips quirked up and the intensity of his gaze softened when he brushed his knuckles over my cheekbone. "You are awake."

With a herculean effort, I took a deep breath and looked away from his knowing gaze, my eyes latching onto anything around the room so I didn't look like a love-sick fool. The tallboy, the side table, the chair, even the thick curtain bunched up on one side of the window so that the star filled night sky was visible through the glass was a better option than staring at Dominic.

"I guess I should've listened to Samir and rested more instead of keeping vigil over Alice. It's not like I could help her." Uncomfortable as hell, I looked at everything but him. "You found me in the hallway?" Switching the subject away from my friend, which was the main cause of discomfort between Dominic and me, I decided to act dumb.

Ignorance was bliss and I clung to it for dear life. I wasn't pretending that nothing happened between us because my memory was all over the place. The erotic images circling around my head could've been a product of my imagination, and for all I knew he found me crumpled on the floor in front of Alice's room.

Okay, fine, I was fishing for information before making an idiot of myself.

"You don't remember anything before you lost consciousness?" The shifter gave a valiant effort to drill a hole into the side of my face with his intense stare.

"Nope." A headache started developing behind my eyes,

and I rubbed them absentmindedly. "I can't afford to allow this to happen, Dominic. Whatever is left of the Syndicate is searching for us and they'll find us sooner or later. Me dropping like a swatted fly could cost us all our lives."

"No one will harm you anymore." The certainty in his voice made me lock gazes with him. "Rowen made a potion that will speed up the process of purging the tainted blood from your system. I should've found you sooner to ask you to take it, but I got sidetracked. It took even longer because you spat out the first mouthful, and I had to hold you down to force you to drink it."

"You mean Rowen's blood." My face twisted in a grimace, remembering the bitter taste of the thick fluid. "I'd rather keep fainting than drinking that again."

"His blood?" Dominic snarled and I jerked away from him instinctively. "You think I would let the witch feed his blood to my mate?"

Awkward silence filled the space between us, dense enough to be cut with a knife.

"Yes?" I tested his anger tentatively, tensed enough to spring out of bed if he tried to grab me. The expression on his face said he wanted to kill someone, and I was the only person within reach. Call me stupid, but I'd rather be prepared to bounce than test the theory mates can't physically hurt each other.

"It was a potion made of tinctures and herbs," he squeezed out between his grinding teeth and hysterical laughter bubbled up in my chest.

After a few snorts, I couldn't hold it back, and I guffawed in his face before slapping a hand over my mouth. A few more giggles and snorts escaped before I could take a breath and control myself.

"Sorry," I told him from between my fingers, not

trusting myself not to laugh again if I removed my hand. "It must be the potion." More giggles followed.

Much to my surprise, he snorted and joined me, his chuckles slow coming but getting louder by the second.

"I couldn't imagine Rowen's face if he were here when I said I thought he gave me his blood." Wiping at my eyes, I scuttled up the bed to sit up straighter. "Poor witch could've tinkled in his robes seeing that glare you gave me."

"You are definitely testing my control, female." All amusement gone, he looked me up and down as if to assure himself that I was not going to collapse again. "I meant what I said before, Brooklyn. Until now, I let you do things your way but that can no longer be the case. My animal will not let me watch you destroy yourself."

"You think I'm trying to hurt myself?" Appalled by his remark, I recoiled from him.

"I didn't say you do it on purpose, I just said I can't sit back and watch anymore. This is me apologizing for getting in the way of your plans from now on." One shoulder rolled in a half assed shrug.

He didn't look sorry at all.

My mouth opened so I could tell him exactly what I thought about it but scratching at the door got both of our attention. I sat up straighter as Dominic irritably rushed to open the door, his legs eating up the space in two long strides. The wolf stuck his head in as soon as the handle was lowered, and one look at the animal had me jumping out of bed and running toward my friend with my mate hot on my heels.

My mate.

It still gave me goosebumps to even think it.

Chapter Four

Chicago had a consistent buzz in the air that you got accustomed to regardless of whether you liked it or not. I rejoiced in it every time the soles of my boots brushed the asphalt of the streets as I joined the sea of humans rushing to reach whatever destination they had in mind. It fascinated me to see them hurry to do everything they set out as a goal for the day. They pushed exhaustion aside as if meeting that person, or buying that loaf of bread, would change their world forever or prevent their life from slipping through their fingers before they had time to blink.

So much tension. So much frustration surrounded them as I passed that it was choking me every time I took a deep breath.

"Excuse me," a middle-aged woman muttered as she bumped into me, her shoulder thumping mine in passing, and as my eyes connected with hers, she recoiled from me wide-eyed, the mane of ash blonde strands lifting around her face as if from static. If I didn't know any better, I would've thought she saw the monster I knew I was behind the youthful face and polite expression.

"You're good." I forced a closed-lipped smile and sped up my steps to get away from her. From all of them, actually. It was on me that I didn't spare a second to check my appearance in the mirror before I left as fast, and as quietly, as I could so the shifter wouldn't see me.

Earlier in the day when Dominic and I rushed to Alice to check on her, I realized that I couldn't just sit around and wait for some miracle to happen. I had to go and find a solution that would help bring my friend back to how she was.

First, however, I had to know if the Council was recovering quickly. Or if luck would heal them slowly enough to give me time to help Alice first. In my bloodlust, I'd caused a lot of damage to the Syndicate. Unfortunately, Isiah and Frederic were very good at hiding behind their goons. So, they were out there somewhere in a hole like some roaches waiting for the right moment to strike. It wouldn't do us any good to find help for Alice just so they could snatch her and use her the way they'd used everyone. She would be better off dead if you asked me.

Samir took it upon himself to take care of my friend; so, I decided to address at a later date the issue of the prophecy he shared with me what felt like a lifetime ago. I had no idea if he told Dominic about it as I asked him, and I hoped he didn't share it with Rowen. It made me sound petty, but I still didn't trust the witch.

There was just something about him.

Ducking in a dark alley between two rundown buildings, I waited for the majority of the crowd to dissipate before I decided that stepping out in the open again was safe. It wasn't very late into the evening, the sun having just set an hour or so ago, and the air was still filled with moisture thick enough to drown you. It was sticking to my lungs with each intake of breath, forcing me to put in an effort just so I could breathe. Leaning my head back on the bricks, I closed my eyes, and for the first time, the sigh passing my parted lips sounded as if all the weight in the world just exited my body. It made me so lightheaded I almost missed the sound coming from the second railing of the fire escape across from me. The second a shoe scraped over the metal everything in me stilled, time slowed down to the point that a blink of an eye became eternity.

Whoever it was realized their mistake at the same time, and they froze, not even taking a breath as we both waited to see what the other would do. I immediately knew my stalker was not human. For the predicament they'd found themselves in, their heart rate was too even when it should have been kicking and punching behind their ribcage. It was also impossible for a human to hold their breath that long without passing out. What set me off the most was the lack of scent.

If I were truthful, I expected Dominic to be his usual stubborn self and nip at my heels the second I snuck out of that cursed house. My stomach dropped at the realization that of all things, I was disappointed he respected my wish to be alone. Something he obviously shouldn't have, judging by the fact the person following me got tired of waiting and dropped into the alley nimbly on her toes while I was stuck with my own thoughts and totally forgot she was there.

Yes, it was a she, which was unmistakable when she was in sight.

If that was a Guardian or some mercenary the Council paid to kill me, I would've been long gone without realizing it.

What in all the worlds was the matter with me?

A tiny slip of a female rose up from her crouch, flicking her long dark braid over her shoulder as she did so. Each movement was loaded with self-confidence, that she was exactly where she needed to be and she had the certainty she would be the one that would walk out of the alley, not me. Misguided as her expectations were, I had to give her credit for first impressions and take a second to truly look her up and down.

Given what I had been through and the fact the Council was searching for me dead or alive, I should've been more careful. But supernatural females were rare and precious. For every ten or more males there was one female. Killing one without a second thought would be the greatest crime of them all. And me?

I was not the Council.

I did not kill without reason even if it was a male.

'Tell that to all those souls you sent to the underworld while you were in bloodlust.' A voice in my head mocked me, souring what little decency I had left in me. I refused to stop clinging to it.

"This is pleasantly surprising." The female yet again yanked me from my thoughts, her voice cultured and crisp like she just answered my request to speak to a representative.

Cocking her head to the side, which made her braid swing like a pendulum over her shoulder, she spoke to me conversationally as if we were two friends meeting up for brunch. I couldn't make out her face since she strategically dropped from the fire escape between me and the exit of the alley, placing her back to the light, but there was no mistaking the body of a warrior. The light glow from the street formed an outline around her forcing me to squint in

25

hopes I could catch the color of her eyes which would've helped me recognize her species. Anything would've helped, really.

Unfortunately, I couldn't see a thing, so I figured I'd play her game for the time being.

"It's usually cooler at this hour, but I would agree with you that it's not horribly hot," I answered, and it worked just as I expected it would.

"I was talking about you, not the weather." She tilted her face sideways and laughed. Enough light broke through to show one side of her face. It passed over the rounded cheekbone, quite long lashes, and the glint of her irises. Her eyes shimmered and brightened for a split second to give her away as a demon.

Taken by surprise, I flinched back, something she didn't miss. All humor left her, and she stiffened, slightly bending her knees in preparation for an attack. My body reacted accordingly, moving my feet slightly apart and relaxing my shoulders so I could move fast if I needed to.

Everything about the situation was off. The Council sent a demon after me? And since I was not trying my best to remove my clothing, she was not a succubus sent to drain the life out of me. I'd heard stories about them but never had the opportunity of meeting one in person. Male or female, it was a very unpleasant way of dying, I'd been told.

"You're a demon," I blurted out, opting for the truth.

"And you are an Atua." She countered, neither accusing me nor judging me for it.

"My guess is the Council sent you to hunt me down, so let's get this over with. I have places to be." With a roll of my shoulders, I took a step toward her.

"They did hire me, but I didn't accept the job so I could kill you." Lifting both hands to her sides, palms up, she countered my movement by stepping back and maintaining the distance between us. "I've been following you for the last few weeks and maintaining my distance because I didn't think you would be willing to stop for a moment and talk. Everything I've learned about you is that you kill first, you check who and what you separated from the land of the living later." Slowly, purposely she turned her body so that I could fully see her. "I thought I was wasting my time trying to chat to tell you the truth."

Chocolate color skin glistened in the light, beautifully outlining the muscles of her toned arms. A leather vest was wrapped around her torso ending an inch above the waist-band of the skin-tight leather pants which looked spray-painted over the legs. There was nothing apart from her long braid that anyone could grab and use against her in a fight. It spoke of experience and promised death to any opponent.

Her demeanor, the tone of her voice, her heart rate and her body language did the right thing though and told me she was speaking the truth. Her only mistake was admitting she accepted a job from the Council. There was not a soul in this world or any other that would risk double-crossing them by agreeing to something and not following through.

She was still turned, her upper body slightly back and to the side, an awkward enough position that would work to my advantage when I struck, and I took the chance. Swiping my foot in a wide arc, I took her feet from under her, following it through with an uppercut punch that caught her chin and whipped her head back. A satisfying crack bounced off of the dirty walls around us, breaking the silence, and I smiled at her grunt when the air left her lungs the second her back hit the ground.

With surprising speed, she was up and backing me into

a corner, her smaller size giving her an advantage. My offensive attack turned into defense, and I hoped I didn't make a mistake of underestimating the demon. My arm hurt every time I deflected her punches, and my shins were bruising from the strength of her kicks. We were moving so fast dust was picking up and forming tiny tornadoes at our feet but neither one of us was backing down. And that was when it happened. For the first time in my life that I could remember, someone managed to best me in a fight.

The female performed a side kick and threw both her hands in front of her the second her feet touched the ground so she was facing me. Red threads of magic burst from her palms and hit me like a ton of bricks at the center of my chest, punching all the air out of me. Searing pain spread through my entire body, and I had no time to think when it knocked me out. The last thought I had was the regret that I would never see Dominic again to tell him how much he meant to me and that I was sorry that I was so damaged that I couldn't be what he needed.

Darkness swallowed me whole.

Chapter Five

DOMINIC

I couldn't tell you what I was thinking to save my life when I heard the crunch of dry leaves coming from behind me. The smooth, glass-like surface of the small pond had yet to erase the last couple of rings from the stone plunging to its depths that I flung at it a second ago. I just stared at the ripples unblinking when whoever it was decided to disturb me. My instincts were calm, so I knew there was no threat coming at me, yet my nature always took over and betrayed me when I wasn't paying attention, or I was deep in thought.

My body tensed, my hand frozen midair, still clutching the next flat, quarter sized rock I picked out of my pocket, and my entire focus zoomed in on the disintegrating leaf under what I was guessing was a size ten shoe. Internally cursing up a storm, I lifted my face and inhaled deep enough to catch the scent of the person who decided to join me. I realized I was atrociously disappointed with the fact that the human was not the one who found me just so she could mock me or annoy me. No, it couldn't be Alice thanks to my lack of ability to save my mate without endangering her friend in the process.

"You are slipping." Rowen stepped out of the shadows like a picture of serenity. His face was tilted at the sky and his eyes closed as if he hadn't been stalking me and watching my every move the last few days. "A reaction like that in front of the wrong people will cost you." He glanced at me from the corner of his eye quickly just to assure himself that he had my undivided attention only to jerk his gaze to the sky when he caught me glaring at him. "It will cost all of us dearly as a matter of fact."

"Thank you, Captain Obvious." My tone came out sharp yet still defensive enough to piss me off. So, I ground my molars hard enough that the nerve-wracking screech of bone on bone made both of us cringe.

"You've been hanging out with the human for too long." A small smile twisted his thin lips, for a moment transforming and softening his harsh features enough to pass as a middle-aged human if you could ignore the glowing sigils on his skin.

I caught myself smiling at that comment too. It was the truth. Alice had been changing all of us, including Samir the ancient oaf, as much as he liked to argue that it wasn't the case.

"Any improvement?" My gut churned and warped, making me nauseous with the reminder that the female was still knocking on Death's door because of me.

"No." All humor drained from his face as he released a heavy sigh and moved to join me while staring at his feet like they had all the answers we needed.

The pebble rolled between my fingers smoothly while I tried to shift my focus from the churning acid in my gut to the repetitive motion of my hand, so I didn't make a fool out of myself and hurl the contents of my stomach at the male's feet. I hadn't felt this weak since I'd found my sister's lifeless body arranged like a broken doll in that field what seemed like a century ago. I still didn't remember her face, no matter how hard I tried. It was blocked by the curtain of midnight strands draping over it. Fingers twitching, my hand started reaching for the past, but I caught myself in time and turned away from Rowen sharply before the witch decided to stick his nose where it didn't belong.

"We must do something." Dropping the pebble on the grass, I rubbed a hand over my face to shake off whatever insanity was trying to possess me. "She won't be able to hold on much longer."

"I'm surprised she's holding on this long." The coarse texture of his robe rasped over the soft cotton of my t-shirt, prickling my skin, when he stopped next to me so close we bumped shoulders. "None of my potions are working for longer than a few hours." He mumbled under his breath low enough for my ears only. "The old Atua is not very happy with me for that reason," the witch added when he saw my raised eyebrow at his lack of respect for personal space.

It made sense he was crowding me; so, Samir did not hear his words, but I still took a deliberate step away from him and narrowed my eyes when I saw the clear debate on his face; if he should move another step closer or stay where he was. Since the day I met him, Rowen had always been a little strange but this was a whole new level of weirdness even for him.

"You fear for your life here?" Turning to face him, I searched his face when he jerked his head so he could stare at me openmouthed and wide-eyed. "And why do you wear that thing?" I tugged at his disgusting robe, barely touching it between two fingers. "You are free to dress however you please now."

"Keep your voice down." Jerking his head left and right to check if anyone was around to hear me, the witch hissed at me after some color returned to his face. Realizing he was acting precariously, he straightened his shoulders and smoothed a hand over the horrible robes. "I need to wear the robes as a reminder of all the rest I left behind. It covers my markings too." He added the last part with a wave of his hand like an afterthought.

"No one will make fun of you for your markings, you know that, right?" My eyebrows pulled down on my fore-head in confusion, wondering if Alice at some point had been facetious and off handedly made a remark that would bother him enough so he would stay hidden.

"Oh, I know." He shook his head as if he couldn't believe I would say something so ridiculous. Before he could cover it up, I caught his hand fisting as he tucked it into the robes. "Everyone has been very nice and kind to me. Although, I do not deserve it."

My snort made him look at me instead of staring at his feet. "Let me guess, we should treat you the same way the Council did to make you feel at home, huh." I almost laughed at his grimace. "What is going on, Rowen? You know you can talk to me no matter what, you are in this position because of me. The least I can do is make sure you are not suffering in your freedom."

I watched the battle play out on his face while he searched by gaze as if debating how much he should disclose. Uneasiness crept up under my skin, wondering if Samir had not left his old ways behind. Had he treated the witch horribly under my nose while I ran around like a besotted fool chasing a female. As I was preparing to keep pushing until he told me what bothered him, he made his decision, and after filling his lungs with more air than they could hold, he chuckled without humor.

"How very appropriate of a description of what I feel." On a sigh, he plopped down on the grass as if his legs could not hold his weight anymore. "Suffering freedom. Isn't that poetic? All of my brothers and sisters would give their lives to trade places with me and here I am *suffering*."

"What is bothering you, old friend. I have been wrapped up in my own problems so much I did not even ask if you are acclimated to your new life. Forgive me for being a lousy friend." Lowering myself next to him, I rested a forearm on my raised knee and stared at the pond, hoping it would make him comfortable enough to share what was going on. Unlike me, the witch was more open to sharing his feelings, although between Brooklyn and Alice, I found myself more attuned to my emotional side as well.

"I still feel the pull." Rowen fidgeted uncomfortably next to me, rearranging his robes mindlessly. "Right here." He thumped a fist over his heart hard enough to crack a bone. "No matter what I do, I still feel the call right here, to return to that place of torment where they imprisoned part of my soul without my consent. Maybe that is why I can't even help the human. My magic is useless." The anguish was evident in the deep lines forming around his eyes and mouth as if what he was describing was causing him physical pain. "I have failed you all."

"That appears to be the theme around here, doesn't it?" Scraping a blunt nail over my calloused palm, I joined in his misery for a moment. "We all feel like we have failed in one way or another. Samir feels he has failed Brooklyn's parents, you think you have failed us all, Brooklyn is guilt ridden for failing Alice, and I have been seeking revenge for so long and drowning in guilt for failing my family that I almost lost my mate when I couldn't think straight because of it." Side-eying him, I could see he was drinking in every word I said. Maybe it was the first time he heard that we were all very much alike. "If you want to take the blame for failing, grab a number and get in line as Alice would like to say."

"I see." Twisting his robes in one hand in an attempt to strangle the life out of the horrendous lifeless thing, he stayed silent for a long moment until he collected his thoughts. "As much as I would like to complain, I must admit having the old…" He cleared his throat and straightened his hunched shoulders. "Having Samir around lessens the uncomfortable feeling of being away from the pits. It is a small price to pay for my freedom."

"Freedom is not free, old friend." Reaching for his shoulder, I gave it a firm squeeze in solidarity and comfort. "We all must pay our dues."

Rowen was slowly nodding his head in agreement, when I felt the first ping of alarm from my animal who had been contentedly letting me have my moment of peace to dwell in my misery after my mate told me to give her some space. It went against everything I was but I forced my legs to move in the direction of the pond, tossing pebbles just so I could occupy my mind with something, anything else, which would give the female what she wanted. Thinking nothing of it, I brushed it away and focused on my friend.

"I wonder if there really is something magical about the human." Rowen switched gears after my speech and was thoughtfully staring into the distance. "Maybe that is why my potions are not working. I am treating her like I would treat the humans at the parties they used to drain to near death. But what if everything I thought about her is wrong?"

"Whatever do you mean?" It was difficult to focus on what he was saying with my animal prowling under my skin, itching to burst out and trade shapes with me. "Alice is human. They all have some remnants of magic in their blood from ancient times when humans were more evolved and could do magic, but they need help from crystals and objects to reach it now. Many never do."

"Yes, but what if we are wrong?" The ridges of his eyebrows almost reached his hairline while excitement sparkled in the glass like the color of his irises. "What if we are totally off about what she is. It could explain everything, couldn't it? It's not like we haven't been wrong about many things before."

"If you treat her like she is supernatural, you could kill her. You know that, right?" I'd be damned if I allowed him to experiment on Alice. Being a fool once and placing her life in danger was enough for a lifetime. Despite being my mate's best friend, I cared about the human, too. "I cannot allow you to do that."

"It could save her life." Rowen stared at me intently enough I began to think he was trying to influence my thoughts. I would've laughed at him if I wasn't feeling light-headed from whatever in the world was happening with the beast inside me.

"No," I ground through clenched teeth.

"Are you well?" The witch grabbed my shoulder to keep me seated when my body tilted sideways. "Your aura is pulsing like you are ready to shift." His eyes widened comically when he heard his words out loud, and he scrambled to get up and get away from me. "Okay, okay, I will not attempt to heal the human like she is one of us. I swear it, I won't."

Curling up on my side on the grass, I couldn't tell him

that whatever was happening had nothing to do with him. Sharp pain cut through me strong enough to make me scream at the skies. My animal was done alerting me that something was not right. It was full of rage and ready to take over because apparently my two-legged side was not paying attention and was oblivious to the danger. All I had time to think about was *'Danger of what?'* when Brooklyn's face floated in my mind's eye, her brilliant green eyes wide and full of regret.

"Brooklyn!" My roar was replaced with a terror inducing cry of my panther as my body shifted instantaneously.

My mate was in danger.

Chapter Six

BROOKLYN

The itch in my ear was persistent to a point of madness but my arm was numb for some reason, and I couldn't scratch it. In the back of my mind, I had a bad feeling about why this was, but I couldn't grasp it long enough to form a cognitive thought. All I knew was I really needed to scratch my ear.

It was driving me insane.

Voices murmured somewhere in the background, yet I paid them no mind. Lately, I had found myself waking up from some injury or being knocked unconscious more times than I could count with Samir, Alice or Dominic mumbling around me about how I have shortened their lives with my recklessness. By some stroke of luck, however, I was still alive.

For some reason I was pretty sure that was not going to change any time soon.

I felt tired to my bones and wanted to sleep.

If only the itching would stop.

"I am not sure irritating her more will work in our best

interest." Whoever the talkaholic was moved close enough to be heard. I was not surprised that it was not a female. And what was it about supernatural males that made them so chatty?

Well, not Dominic. He was all broody and silent, but he was a feline. It was his nature. The rest, however, couldn't hold their tongues to save their lives. Like the chatterbox here that kept at it without realizing the moment my arms stopped being numb I would have my hands wrapped around his neck.

After I was done scratching the damn ear.

"I would honestly stop that." The male's raspy tone irked me more. "It looks like she's coming around."

'It sounds to me like you are afraid of her, Chester." A female purred so close to my itchy ear her breath added to the tickling as it brushed my skin. Mockingly clicking her tongue, she gave me goosebumps when she spoke. "Are you scared of the Atua, little Chip?" My whole body became tense and on alert when she chuckled. "Don't you worry. I will protect you."

"I doubt you will be in a position to help anyone including yourself if you don't move away from me." My words came off a little raspier than I would've liked if my threat was to be taken seriously, but I had to go with the flow and take things as they were. Alice was rubbing off on me.

And I still couldn't open my eyes. It felt like I had sandpaper instead of eyelids.

"Marvelous." The female sounded truly in awe while I doubled my efforts. "She is truly about to break the hold of my magic."

"I hope she can hear us because I would love for her to know that I had nothing to do with this and that you are unstable." The male barely took a breath as his voice moved further away from me. "Whatever grievances she has, she should be taking it up with you."

"You are afraid, Chip. It is a rare treat to see you so pale." The female laughed with glee. "I'm half tempted to remove the hold I have on her just to see you quiver and shake." Her irritating laugh stopped abruptly when I muttered under my breath. "What did you say?"

"I said"—lifting my head from where it rolled limply on my shoulders so she could hear me better, I grinned blindly in the direction I thought she was in—"there are over a million words in the human language we speak, but I can never string enough words together to properly express how much I want to hit you with a chair."

"I told you it's a bad idea," the male mumbled to his nose. "She may not be with the Syndicate, but they raised her. Now you and I are juicy bones between two rabid dogs." His voice kept getting higher in pitch. "We are going to die." As soon as the hyperventilating stopped, he whispered dramatically. "Very painfully."

"Knock it off, Chester." High heels clicked over tiles as she moved around me, and I tracked her with my head since my eyes were still glued shut. "I'm not releasing her until she promises that she will hear me out first. I know you can hear us."

The memory from the alleyway came clear as day in my mind while she talked, and I stilled, anger bubbling instantly inside me. "You have a funny way of getting someone's attention if talking is all you want to do. Try a phone call to arrange a meeting next time. I'm not an expert on interactions but I'd guess it works better than an attack in a dark alley." My shoulders squared, and it sent a sharp pain traveling up my arms. Which told me my arms were numb because I was hanging by my tied wrists.

"Exactly what I told her." Chester mumbled from somewhere to my right.

"Shut it, Chip." The female barked at him. "Two of my brothers tried talking reason with you and ended up drained of blood and tossed like trash on the streets of Chicago. I had no intention of parting with my lifeforce to get a minute of your time while you were on a killing spree."

My indignation dwindled to nothing when I heard I killed members of her family. The fact she kept me alive was a miracle now that she put it that way. Not remembering coming across not one but two demons told me she was speaking the truth, and it happened while I was in bloodlust. I curbed my rage and decided to hear her out. If she wanted to kill me when she spoke her piece, I couldn't say I would blame her.

I'd kill me too if I were her.

Not like I would let it happen, but I totally understood where she was coming from if she wanted to try.

I needed one thing first before she started venting. I might have been a monster, but cowardly I was not. I would look her in the eye when she called me every name on earth for destroying her family.

"Release me from your hold so I can look at you," I told her as calmly as I could muster it. "You can leave me tied up, but I would like to look you in the eye when I tell you how sorry I am for killing your brothers. You need to see I'm telling the truth."

"Well, I'd be damned," Chester said on a breath.

"You *are* damned, you idiot. You're a demon," the female muttered but I could feel her studying me, her gaze heavy on the skin of my face.

The weight holding my eyelids lifted without another word from any of them, and I slowly opened my eyes, first glancing through my lashes in case they decided to jab me with something the moment I blinked, then fully stretching my lids to clear my vision.

It took me a second to comprehend what I was seeing, and then I blinked a few times rapidly as if that might change the scene. A very domestic type of scene, a total opposite of the dark blood-soaked dungeon feel I had when my sight was taken.

"This is kind of nice." I heard myself saying as I examined the pale blue gauzy drapes on the windows whose blinds were tightly closed.

Pictures in pretty frames were sprinkled over dressers and side tables as well as hanging on the walls. Modern, uncomfortable-looking furniture sat at the center of a large living room with me hanging in one corner of it like a long-forgotten Christmas decoration somebody thought it'd be funny to keep year-round. What got my full attention however was the white fluffy rug under the low, oval-shaped glass table. It was so white, it hurt to look at it.

"We might want to take this to another room." I told the two demons absentmindedly, unable to look away from the rug. "Do you have a basement in this house maybe?" When they didn't answer, I forced my gaze from the rug to look at them. "No?"

Chester was shaking his head in agreement and was a real surprise with his physical appearance, which was a contradiction to his fearful comments. I must've become judgmental somewhere along the line if my expectations were the opposite of reality. That was not a problem I'd had before.

"Why do you need a basement?" the demon asked and

narrowed his gaze in suspicion as if I was asking him some trick questions. Muscles rippled under his tight long-sleeved shirt when he folded his beefy arms across his chest. "You agreed to only talk if Echo released you from the hold of her magic. We also have wards around the house, no one can hear us."

Assuming he was talking about the female when he called her Echo, I turned my eyes on her, and our gazes locked. It was the same female that followed me in the alley, with her long braid draped over one shoulder and her chocolate skin shimmering under the light of the room. A silver sheen flickered over her irises as she watched me, assessing me as I was assessing her. Begrudgingly, I had to nod in respect to the warrior. I could tell she was surprised that she reciprocated in kind.

"I assumed you want to kill me." I told them both honestly. "The blood won't wash off that rug." Chester stared openmouthed at me while Echo cocked her head in puzzlement like she couldn't figure out my angle. "It's white." I said slowly in case they were color blind or something.

Are demons color blind? Embarrassingly enough I realized I knew next to nothing about their kind.

"You are sure she is the one that killed our brothers?" Chester continued to gawk at me, and my mouth twisted in disapproval of the insult.

"I thought you wanted to talk not insult each other." And just because I wanted them to understand who had control of the situation so there was no more mistaking who would walk out of here alive if it came to that, I took a deep breath and used my voice to compel someone just as a power play tool. "Release my arms."

The chains holding my arms up dropped to my feet with

a loud clinking of metal against metal, and I gingerly took a hold of my wrists to rub off the pain. Circulation was slowly returning to them, and I had to grind my teeth at the ant sensation crawling all the way up to my shoulders.

"Now, let's talk." On a heavy sigh I took a few steps to the closest armchair and plopped into it. "A glass of water would be nice, too."

Chapter Seven

DOMINIC

Gasping for air, I clawed the damp grass under my fingers until I could catch my breath and look around to see where I ended up. There was a black hole in my memory from the moment I talked to Rowen at the pond to shifting in the park, and luckily for me, an abandoned street was the only witness to my madness. All I could recall was the pain ripping through my body and forcing my animal to take over my human form.

After that the bastard blocked me.

Glaring at the night, I hope he knew how mad I was. My beast was acting as if Brooklyn was his mate and not mine. She was the most important person in my life, too. If she were in danger, I needed my brain to function so I could get her out of it instead of acting on animal instinct and getting both of us killed.

The disapproval of my beast was evident in the pressure at the back of my head. He wanted to trade forms and wasn't shy about it. The fact it took me forever to push him out of the way so I could see where he was taking me, made sure I stayed alert and ready to fight the shift if it started again.

"Was there a particular reason you brought us here?" hearing Samir speak from a couple of feet behind me almost made me jump out of my skin.

"You could die sneaking up on me like that." Whirling around, I scowled in his direction. "Why are you here? You're supposed to protect and take care of Alice."

"Rowen was beside himself thinking you are about to divorce half of Chicago from their lives. I had to rush in case I had to do damage control." After staring daggers at me for the longest time to relay his message of annoyance, the ancient Atua rolled his gaze over the sparse trees and patches of almost dried out grass around us with disgust. "We are too close to reaching our goal and destroying the Syndicate for you to mess it up now. So, I shall ask again. Was there a particular reason you brought us here?"

"Brooklyn is in danger."

"I do not see Brooklyn here." Speaking slowly, he studied me like you would someone who was not of sound reasoning. "Let me ask again. Where is Brooklyn?" He glowered at me down his nose. "We are all adults, and we need to know when to run around like insolent children and when to stop and think about the consequences. I thought we all agreed we have a common goal. Maybe I should rethink my involvement and find other ways to deal with the Council. All these complications are making us chase our tails instead of making a solid plan. This nonsense needs to stop."

"You should go and protect the human, Samir." Pushing the words through clenched teeth, I yanked down my T-shirt where it crawled up my torso. "I doubt that Brooklyn will do something reckless, but it's stronger than me. I need to make sure that she's well. My animal is restless, warning me that she's in danger, but I doubt that after everything she has gone on her own to hunt anyone from the Syndicate."

Rubbing a fist over my chest, I tried to dispel the uneasy feeling that was wrapping around my insides, making it difficult to breathe regardless that I tried to sound confident and calm for Samir's sake. I was well aware that my animal would not be doing this if Brooklyn was not in danger.

My mate needed me, and I needed to be there for her.

Just as Samir opened his mouth to say something, and I was gearing up to reply in not so many nice words, a squealing sound of tires over concrete reached our ears. We both turned to see the vehicle sharply take the corner, and instead of continuing down the street, it headed right in our direction. Lights blinded me, so I had to throw my arm in front of my face out of instinct. A second later, Samir slammed his body into me and tackled me to the ground hard enough that we cracked the nearest tree when it stopped our rolling.

The vehicle crashed through the poor excuse of a fence and plowed through trees and shrubbery alike until the person driving it yanked on the steering wheel hoping to point it at us again. The car rose on two wheels, teetering precariously for a long moment before dropping on all four tires and pitching forward right at the small fountain sitting unassumingly a few yards away. Marble cracked a second before a loud hiss came from the hood of the car as it scrunched up on impact and a large cloud of smoke puffed up above it.

Samir and I stared at it stunned, still sprawled in the dirt and dead leaves until the doors on both sides opened and four Guardians spilled out of it, swords already drawn out and ready to slice into us.

Pushing the ancient Atua off of me and rolling up on my feet, I barely had time to duck before the first male was on me, his longsword singing through the air a quarter of an inch above my head. A cold wave washed over me, numbing my arms and weakening my knees. Was this the reason my animal was mindless with fear for our mate? Did they capture Brooklyn first and now were attacking us.

I didn't attempt to stand up and face the male. Staying hunched over, I took a deep breath and tackled him. Not expecting a wrestling match from a shifter, my action took him by surprise. All the air came out of him in a loud whoosh, and he cried out when his back hit the ground with my full weight on top of him.

In the background, I could hear the grunts and snarls from Samir fighting his own two opponents accompanied by the breaking of trees and chunks of dirt and soil flying through the air. I wanted to check on him and make sure there were not more than two Guardians he had to deal with, but a sharp pain in my arm got my undivided attention. A sword was embedded in my bicep, the hilt firmly clutched in the beefy fingers of the Guardian glaring down at me.

"You need to die." He snarled and yanked the blade through my flesh slow enough to bring dancing stars in front of my eyes.

"Sorry to disappoint." Grunting the words from the pain which was making me nauseous, I rolled away before he could stab at me again. "I have a few more things to get done before I meet my maker."

"Stop playing around and kill him," the second Guardian spat as he was finally able to get some air into his lungs. "Kill the scum."

The words were barely out of his mouth when Samir's foot connected to the side of the Guardian's head and the crunch of a neck breaking echoed and bounced off the remaining trees around us. "If you are done messing around..." The ancient Atua raised a haughty eyebrow at me, looking like the stick up his ass never moved even in a dirty fight in the middle of a dog park.

"I'm trying not to shift." Pissed at myself for showing vulnerability, I shoved off the dirt and stood up.

"Shifting would be a good thing in a situation like this." Side-eyeing me, Samir twisted and turned to avoid the Guardian's sword and fists. "I do not have time for this."

"I didn't ask for your assistance, Samir." Anger pushed away any hesitation I had in releasing control of my temper. "Need I remind you that you are here uninvited?"

"And you are welcome for the assistance I offered, although you were too dimwitted to ask." It was beyond me how he managed the elaborate arm roll in his bow at the same time he slammed a fist into the only remaining Guardian in the park. "While the adults deal with the vermin, do tie something around that well of Muscat pouring out of your arm, would you? It smells vintage, and after fighting all of the Guardians on my own I'm getting famished." Twisting his head to face me, he grinned wide enough to expose both of his sharp fangs at me.

Even knowing that he was on our side, I was still more wary of Samir than anything else that could come and try to kill me in this park. With a cocked eyebrow, I glanced down at my bleeding bicep, the blood painting my skin all the way down to my fingertips. Without a word, I tugged the t-shirt over my head and started ripping into it to get a long enough piece and tie it above the injury to cut off the circulation. Arguing with the Atua wouldn't lead me to anything good.

With a few more grunts and huffs, the last Guardian hit the ground and lay unmoving. Samir smoothed a hand over his button-down shirt to erase the invisible wrinkles while I tightened the knot on the ripped fabric with my teeth, half paying attention to what I was doing, half watching the Atua in case he needed assistance. Those damn blades the Syndicate started using healed too slow even for a shifter. It would be a day before the wound fully closed and that would be a problem if the Syndicate had my mate.

How did you investigate anything when they could smell you bleeding from miles away?

"Did you break a claw, Shifter?" Samir smirked down at me, and I glowered back.

"We should check if they have Brooklyn in the vehicle." Without waiting for his reply, I strode toward the still smoking car that was half wrapped around the fountain.

She wasn't there. Or anywhere near this damn place. I knew it, yet I forced myself to check in hopes I'd keep my sanity. Why did my beast lead me here where no sign of her could be found?

Behind me, Samir was dragging bodies, rearranging them around the park to make it look like they had been fighting each other and ended up all dead. Unlike me. I stared unseeing at the open doors of the car, the interior clean and still smelling of new leather.

"Anything?" Samir called out from a few yards away.

Shaking my head since I knew he could see me, I was just turning around to join him when a strong gust of wind blasted from the empty street through the park, slamming me with the scent of my mate; it was like being hit with a hammer. It brought her smell from across the street not the park. It was all my animal needed to shove me out of the way and take over.

I shifted with a shout of outrage and heard Samir laugh. Asshole.

Chapter Eight

BROOKLYN

Stuck in a staring match with two demons in a living room set of a typical middle-class American family was surreal. My eyes flicked from Echo to Chester, hoping that each time I blinked I'd wake up in Samir's estate and all this would be a dream. More to suit my ego that I couldn't possibly be kidnaped like some rookie human than from the fear that I might lose my life in a house from an episode of House Hunters that Alice made me watch when we were not too busy running or fighting for our lives.

"Well?" When the silence stretched for too long I raised an eyebrow at my two captors.

Echo narrowed her gaze on me, a muscle ticking on one side of her jaw in annoyance while the male demon was unnerving with his excited fascination with me. Regardless, if the female found me annoying or not, I kept a steady look on my face, displaying patience I didn't feel. She was the one that wanted to talk, while I really wanted to be out of there. Had places to be and Atua to kill.

"How much do you know about the breeding of a new species so the Syndicate can build their army?"

I blinked.

As far as opening statements went, I had to give credit to Echo. The female screeched my scattered brain to a stop and had my undivided attention with just that one question. A quick look at Chester told me absolutely nothing since he was still either eye-fucking me or debating if he should start eating me from the head or the legs the second I was dead.

A shiver ran up and down my spine, and I trembled for a second.

"Nothing." Clearing my throat, I straightened in the armchair. "Since you are the one that does business with the Council…" I pointedly looked at my sore wrists I was rubbing so I could return some of the feeling in my fingers "…you should know they are not exactly forthcoming with information on anything, little less on something I'm assuming they want to have as an ace up their sleeve."

If there was a war brewing in the shadows and we were running around clueless, Samir and Dominic were going to be very upset. It would explain why they were so quick to try and get rid of me though. From the moment I was captured and shoved in a cage, I expected a lot more torture and blood loss. Not wanting to look a gift horse in the mouth, I didn't give it a second thought when I got rescued if it was too easy or not. Having a witch from the inside to help made it possible to believe we managed to trick the Council and strike unexpected.

But what if we were wrong?

"We've been watching you, Brooklyn, long before you turned on the Syndicate." Echo leaned a hip on the sofa and folded her arms across her chest. "They treated you like one of their own. You were part of the inside circle for a long time. You must know something."

"I know some things like why your brothers were killed." Not very tasteful, but I had to cut to the chase. "I was not in my right mind, and I can only guess that they were in the wrong place at the wrong time. From what I've been told, I only killed members of the Syndicate. You are the first that tells me otherwise." Shrugging a shoulder, I held her gaze levelly. "I am sorry for that, but I cannot get it undone."

"Maybe we should start from the beginning." Chester finally decided to join the conversation. Plopping onto the sofa he leaned forward, rubbed his face on a sigh like the weight of the world was on his shoulders and placed his forearms on his knees. The more he spoke the larger the pit in my stomach formed and all the blood was draining from my body. By the time he rehashed the last few months they could've pushed me from the armchair with a feather.

"A few years back demons started to go missing." Pausing long enough to side-eye Echo in case he angered her with his retelling, Chester continued his story. "At first, we didn't think anything of it, but when other species started to hire mercenaries to look for missing members we looked more closely into the disappearances. All the missing males were in prime health conditions, and they all vanished from the face of the Earth."

I thought Echo was going to shut him up, but she sluggishly moved and sat next to him before adding in barely a whisper, "No sign of any of them. No one had seen or heard anything. All of them were keeping their heads low and none were looking for trouble. Especially with the Syndicate. We all know what comes from messing with you lot. And the Council laughed at us when we asked for an audience with them. Mocked us even."

"We knew it was futile, but we had to try." Chester bumped his shoulder on hers affectionately. "But we did notice the looks they gave each other, and we started investigating further. Their arrogance gave away their involvement."

"The Council has done many unforgivable things." On a chance that I would sound rude, I had to push them to tell me what the point was of my kidnaping or we would've stayed there for days telling stories. "Echo, you said you accepted the job of killing me in hopes to talk to me. Unfortunately, I have unfinished business with the Syndicate, and I cannot allow you to complete your part of the deal. Which means they already have someone hunting for you as we speak."

"We had someone enter the cages while you were there," Chester rushed to say before Echo could speak. "We know you saw the abominations you had to fight. They shouldn't have existed yet, there they were. And they were not the only ones. In the last six months we gathered enough information to be certain every missing male is taken in the pit, and they are being used for experimentation in creating the Syndicate army."

My mouth opened and closed a few times, but no words came out. At the end I leaned back in the armchair and watched the two demons mutely. Many things floated through my mind so I could argue with them and tell them it was not my problem but was that the truth? Could I turn a blind eye on this new information they shared when I knew first-hand how difficult it was to fight the mangled creatures Frederic was hoping would kill me?

"Army for what?" was all I could dumbly ask to stall until I can wrap my mind around everything. "The Syndicate terrorizes everyone anyway. What do they need mutants for?"

"All we managed to hear was they are preparing in case some prophecy comes to pass."

All the blood drained from my body and tingles spread through my extremities. "Prophecy?" I mouthed and they both nodded gravely.

"Yeah." Echo said on a sigh. "Some very overfull witch is supposed to resurface that will create a new world order and the Council is gearing up to stop that from happening." She eyed me for a second. "We are not making this up. We have no hidden agenda. The lives of my brothers are a testament to that. Brooklyn"—she leaned forward, reached over the table for my hands and squeezed my fingers tightly —"we are desperate. They started taking our females now. I think to breed them with those things."

Bile filled my mouth and fear clawed at my insides. The raspy, raw voice of my savior from the cage next to mine came to torment me. Was it a female? Was that her fate if we did nothing? To breed with those abominations so she could populate the Council's army? And if we did nothing what would happen to me or Alice when eventually the Syndicate became too powerful to conquer?

"We need your help, Brooklyn." Echo clutched at my fingers. "We've seen what you can do and how you dispose of them. Please. I'm begging you. We will pay anything you ask. Give you anything you desire."

"Anything," Chester added, his eyes shimmering silver as he watched me solemnly.

"I don't want payment." A million thoughts were zipping through my head. Were the murders they ordered me to commit on the shifters connected somehow?

"There must be something we can offer in exchange for your help. Please." Echo dropped on her knees in front of me, and for the first time I could see beyond the warrior exterior she worked hard to portray. I saw the desperate, broken woman beneath. "Please." Tears shimmered at the corners of her silvery eyes. "They took my little sister a week ago."

"I didn't say I will not help, Echo." The hope that bloomed in her upturned gaze broke my heart anew. "I said I do not need a payment." Glancing from her to Chester, I made sure they could see my determination. "We need to go and tell all of this to Dominic and Samir. We will help you find your sister before it's too late. And I have every intention of stopping the Council before they can destroy any more lives."

"Thank you." Echo dropped her head on a sob, but we had no time for sentiments like that.

"We need to go." Jumping to my feet I pulled her up with me. "Grab anything you need, we are leaving. You two can stay with us for now until we have a solid plan."

Watching the two of them rush around stuffing things in backpacks, I paced the room. The prophecy they mentioned was the same one Samir told me about that involved Alice and my mother. It was important now more than ever to finish what we started. The Council must die.

"We are ready," Chester called out from the front door down the hallway.

"Maybe you'll know how to help my friend," I told them as I followed them out the front door." If they had an idea about the situation with Alice, it would be an added bonus.

"Anything you need," Echo told me.

"If we can't, we will find someone that can," Chester added.

I wasn't so sure, but I still hoped.

Chapter Nine

BROOKLYN

What is it about males that the moment you leave them alone they manage to cause so much trouble and you are left with the dilemma if you should laugh from the insanity of it or strangle them because you are too mad to argue?

There I was, bringing not one but two demons to our present safe house—if we could call Samir's multilevel monstrosity of a house that—and instead of being grateful that I'm at least trying to come up with a solution to our current problem, they glower at me. It didn't faze me a bit, but I would've appreciated a little more enthusiasm for my efforts.

Which, I told them, in not so many words.

Okay, fine, it was more in the style of "say a word and I'll rip your throat out," but still. I communicated my displeasure.

"Is there an explanation for the additional guests you brought, Brooklyn?" Samir narrowed his gaze on me from the top of the stairway the moment I entered the house. He broadened his stance and folded his arms like some sentinel of the mansion, I'm guessing so he could look more threatening.

"They have information we need, and they need our help." Not pausing in my advance toward him, I waved to the two demons to follow me when they both froze a foot inside the door. "Is there a problem?" I asked them when they stayed frozen, staring at Samir. You'd think they'd seen a ghost.

"I expected you to be many things, Brooklyn." Echo hissed at me, betrayal clouding her silvery eyes. "Liar was not one of them."

Confused, I watched her turn back-to-back with Chester who also looked like I stole his favorite toy and refused to lock eyes with me. The shock of all surprises was when I realized they were preparing to fight. I was about to tell Samir to get lost and go work on his manners when the words got stuck in my throat. The demons were not acting strange because of what Samir said. They were being weird because Samir was here. I guess they had no clue the Council lost one member not that long ago. I didn't know if that was a good sign, meaning we were one step ahead of whatever war was brewing in our city, or a bad sign that our new friends were not as informed as they wanted me to believe.

But I didn't have them with me for the Council.

I needed them for Alice.

Echo lifted her arm, palm cupped and ready to lob magic toward Samir. And although the arrogant male could've used a wake-up call and a notch down from his high horse, I had to stop them before they outright started fighting and someone ended up getting seriously hurt.

"Echo, stop." Placing myself between her and Samir, I lifted both my hands in a universal sign for peace. "Samir has been helping us fight the Council. He is no longer one of them." I also hoped with everything in me that I was telling the truth.

Did Samir help us? Yes, absolutely. Did he have a hidden agenda I knew nothing about? He was an ancient Atua, former member of the Council. I'd be a fool to think he didn't. Until I was sure of what that agenda was, however, I had to make sure he was safe around me. The fact he had a soft spot for Alice also worked in his favor.

"Just because he decided to take a break from tormenting and killing for the time being, it does not make him a friend." Echo spat in the direction of Samir who was looking down his nose at her with one cocked eyebrow and a sneer playing on his lips.

Dominic stood to the side, arms folded over his chest and an unimpressed sour expression plastered all over his handsome face. Guilt drilled a hole in me that although I was acting unreasonable toward him, he still respected my wishes and stood aside without getting involved. I had to fix the problem I created with my mate, but it was not the right time for it.

"I'm not asking you to be friends with him." Sliding to the left, I made sure Echo had her attention more on me than Samir.

Doing my best to placate the demon and keep the situation under control, I kept my tone even, pushing aside all thoughts of my horrible decision making when it came to relationships. Fingers crossed I wouldn't have to use my curse to get Echo to back down. Once using it against them could be explained with lies and mumbo-jumbo. A second time would be a tough cookie to swallow.

"You needed my help. Remember?" Resorting to blackmail, I shrugged when her gaze narrowed on me. "This is not some sort of a trap that I tricked you into following. You attacked and kidnapped me in that alley…"

And that's how all hell broke loose. Dominic shifted before I could take a breath to tell him to calm down and pounced on the closest demon to him. Chester appeared to be expecting it and the two of them crashed with the slapping sound of fists and claws smashing into flesh and bones.

Samir slid down the railing like some Frank Sinatra double ready to start singing under an umbrella, his polished loafers clicking on the marble floors in the entryway when he executed a perfectly graceful landing. Echo bolted like a bullet for him, ruffling the hairs that escaped my ponytail a second before they slammed into each other. Magic boomed from one of the demons strong enough that the foundation of the structure shook under my boots.

I closed my eyes on a groan.

Was it too much to ask for things to go smoothly for once.

Rubbing my face tiredly, I stepped aside and let the four of them get their frustration out for a while. I mean, it wasn't me hurting at the end of the day. I had every intention of asking all of them if it was worth it when they smarted bruises later.

A tail thick and long like rope swung for my head, and I ducked at the last moment, saving my face from one of the bruises I wanted to gloat about everyone else having later. It smashed into an unassuming vase sitting on top of a Greek style column bursting it into thousands of sharp shards which promptly sliced into the exposed skin of my arms. With a hiss, I spun around, avoiding the rest but not before Dominic heard it. A loud roar of a pissed off feline shook the glass on all the windows and doors, pausing the fighting long enough for all of them to see me bleeding all over the marble.

"Shit." Chester had barely enough time to gape at me before the panther ripped into him with teeth and claws. I had to do something, or Dominic was going to kill the poor demon for hurting me.

"Dominic, no!" My shout did nothing, but I followed it fast with action, throwing myself on the panther and wrapping my body around him. "Stop! You'll kill him."

Another cry bounced off the walls filled with so much pain and confusion my heart broke for Dominic and his animal. I had no doubt the beast couldn't understand how he could hurt his mate instead of protecting me. Instead of allowing Dominic to switch places with him and come to the surface, he channeled it into rage and kept trying his best to get his claws and teeth into Chester. Samir and Echo were not spared any bruises either, since the panther was in a frenzied anger. The large body was bouncing from walls and anything else in his way in his attempt to kill his opponent. Echo ended up in a heap at the foot of the stairway, Samir jumped out of the way, practically levitating himself halfway up the railing where he clutched the banister like he was imagining it was Dominic's neck. It would've been funny if the situation was not dire.

If the panther didn't shift soon, he would do irreversible damage to the demon who'd started bleeding profusely all over the entryway.

"Dominic, stop!" Desperately clinging to his thick neck, I tucked my face in his silky coat as I resorted to begging the animal to see reason. "It's just a scratch, I promise. It's already healed and if you stop, you'll see it for yourself. You need to stop, Mate."

Everything stopped at once. Harsh breathing coming

from Chester was the only sound slicing the eerie silence. The panther stood frozen mid-step, one paw lifted to the side as he prepared himself to take another chunk from the demon's back.

Carefully, so I didn't startle him with sudden movements, I slid off Dominic's back and found myself kneeling in a pool of Chester's blood. A puff of air stirred the baby hairs on my hairline a second before a thick raspy tongue slobbered all over my face from neck to my forehead. Soft chirps followed it, and I forced myself not to grimace at the fact my face was covered in panther saliva.

He bumped his head on my shoulder so I could look at him and proceeded to search my gaze when we locked eyes. It was unnerving, but I knew what he was asking. He wanted me to address him as mate again while he was looking at me.

"You and I have always gotten along much better than me and Dominic, Mate." Remembering how much I wished he was there before I lost consciousness in the alley I smiled sadly at him. "I'm sorry I've been difficult after you did everything in your power to save me. I'll try to do better, but I do need Dominic right now so he can help me sort out this mess."

Aware that the other three were watching us, I fidgeted where I knelt, the thickening blood squelching under me. I tentatively reached out a hand and scratched behind his ear. Immediately, those piercing green eyes narrowed, and I jerked back, praying I didn't mess it up and upset him.

"As much as I would rather have you kill the demons, Shifter." Samir came around to himself finally and pushed off the railing he had been clutching tightly. "I'm dying to hear the explanation for all this. It's not every day Brooklyn brings visitors to my home so they could attempt to kill me."

The ancient Atua lifted an arrogant eyebrow at my deadpan look, not that I had any ground to stand on if I wanted to argue. He was correct. I did bring the demons into his house, and they did attack him without provocation. I should've expected it, given the fact they wanted my help to kill the rest of the Council and get their people back. It just never occurred to me they had no clue Samir was mercurial in nature. I fully expected him to turn on us the moment he thought we were the losing side.

While I was stuck in my own head, Dominic made his appearance, the shift seemingly a breeze from how smooth it always went. The breath caught in my throat when I looked up from his powerful thighs to his washboard abs pushing against the fabric of his shirt, over the mouthwatering chest, to his smoldering gaze. Good thing I was kneeling like a peasant at his feet because my legs got weak from the intensity in his eyes.

"Here I am, Mate." The deep, raspy tone of his voice vibrated in my lower belly, and like a fledgling, I had to press my thighs closed and bite the inside of my mouth not to whimper. "Let us hear the reason for the presence of the demons who have tried to harm you. That way I can decide if I should allow my beast to return and finish what he started."

"You can't blame them for kidnapping me." With a sigh, I raised my hand so I could rub the tiredness off my face but stopped midway when I saw all the blood and dirt smudged on it. Instead, I wiped it on my pants with a grimace. "I killed two of Echo's brothers when they tried to talk to me while I was in bloodlust."

"I'm still not convinced it was smart bringing them here." Samir spoke to me but he was glaring at Echo who was picking herself up off the floor.

"They know why we had to fight abominations when you rescued me from the cages." It made me happy to see Dominic's mouth form an "oh" and he looked at the two demons in a whole new light.

"I need help, right now." Rowen stuck his head out from the hallway upstairs and everything we'd been doing or saying was forgotten.

"Alice!" I grabbed the hand Dominic offered to jump to my feet and we rushed to the bedroom my friend was in. I hoped she was not getting worse.

With my heart drumming in my throat and fear like I'd never felt before, I was first to dart inside the room.

Chapter Ten

BROOKLYN

Rowen blinked his faded eyes at me as if I were speaking in tongues. Anger bobbled up fast and hot from his blank expression, but I had to push it down, so I didn't do something foolish, like kill the witch. I guess he was aware that he was in danger because the sigils on his skin were turning into a light show, the frequency of how fast they glowed increasing by the second.

"What did you do to her?" I repeated through clenched teeth, gripping the seams of my pants so I didn't wrap them around his neck.

"Ummm..." Rowen's gaze dropped to his feet as he shuffled them before darting all around the room. Nervous energy was coming off of him in waves, blasting all of my senses.

Clusters of half-melted candles sat all over the room, the wax forming abstract shapes on the floor around them. Crystals were sprinkled strategically in the four corners to represent each element closing a circle. What truly worried me, and I did my best to pretend I didn't see it, was the pinkish stuff over the salt, which was used to paint the pentagram under Alice.

Oh, yeah. My friend was not resting on the soft mattress and fluffy pillows like I left her. She was placed on the floor on top of said pentagram like some satanic virgin sacrifice, her hands neatly folded over her sternum and her chestnut hair fanned around her head like a halo. Even her glasses were perched on her freckled nose so tidily that if she wasn't on the ground I would've thought she was dead. Alice was never one to have everything set up perfectly about her, especially not those glasses.

"Answer my mate." Dominic growled menacingly from behind me, the heat of his body warming my entire back. "I told you not to mess with the human, Rowen. I will shred you to pieces if you have harmed her."

Samir had no desire to talk or ask questions. When his attempt to reach Alice failed and he comically bounced off of whatever protection the witch had placed, he simply walked around the four of us crowding the doorway, and upon reaching Rowen, he lifted him by the neck.

"Break the circle." The ancient Atua shook the witch like he was a ragdoll, not a grown male. "Now!" After baring his fangs, he also hissed in case anyone missed how furious he was.

"No," Rowen croaked, clawing at Samir's fingers and gasping for air. "It's working. I can't breathe."

"Of course it's working, you insolent worm. I'm choking you." The elder snarled, spittle flying from his mouth. "Break the magic this instant."

As much as I wanted to join Samir and help him kill Rowen, I had to stifle my anger for my friend's sake. As for Dominic. I could feel the shifter vibrating behind me, and I had no doubt he was on the brink of changing shape and was barely holding back.

Instead of feeding into their anger, I closed my eyes and blocked everyone out. Focusing on Alice, I tried to check how my friend was doing. What reached my ears was something totally unexpected. A steady, strong heartbeat was rhythmically distributing blood through her body. Excited to share what I heard, my eyes snapped open and a gasp of horror was ripped from my chest.

"Samir, release him!"

For the second time that day, I used the power of my voice to force someone to do something, and it didn't sit well with me. Bile rose, filling my mouth with a bitter taste. I could justify it by saying Rowen was turning purplish blue in the face, and his heartbeat was barely there, but I didn't have to use the damn curse. I could've slapped Samir away from the witch. Dominic would've happily helped, I'm sure.

The shifter was itching to hit something at that point.

"Have you lost your ever-loving mind!" Samir turned his rage on me. Not that I could blame him. "First you bring demons that try to kill me in my own house, now you want to test who is more powerful between the two of us? You are crossing every line, child."

Rowen, however, was giving me grateful glances from the floor where he was dropped while he was rubbing his neck. Bruises in the shape of Samir's long fingers were appearing darker and darker by the second.

"We can do whatever you want, Samir." Not taking the bait to get into an argument, I pointed at my friend lying motionless in the magic circle. "For a moment stop talking and listen to her heartbeat. Whatever he did"—jutting my chin toward Rowen —I didn't return his tentative smile—"it works. Listen."

"I managed to stabilize her." Rowen shakily pushed himself off the floor as Samir kneeled as close to Alice as he could without touching the circle.

Dominic and I looked at each other.

"She was even awake to speak with me for a short while. Unfortunately, we got excited too fast, and I dropped the circle so we could both come and tell you the spell worked and that your friend is well." Confusion clouded Rowen's features, and much to my surprise, the witch stepped close to where Samir was listening to Alice's heartbeat with his eyes closed. Pure relief was etched across his face. "The second the circle broke, she dropped lifeless on the floor. I panicked and opened the circle back up immediately."

"Was she awake after you opened it?" It was the first time Echo spoke, shocking me to hear her voice, because I totally forgot the two demons were in the room with us.

She was watching the area where Alice was sleeping through a slanted gaze, as if she could see something the rest of us couldn't. Placing a hand on Dominic's forearm, I stepped aside, taking him with me, giving her more room in case she had an insight that could help.

"That's the thing." Tone full of frustration, Rowen started slapping his robe to clean it from whatever dirt, dried herbs, and dust it had collected from the floor. "As soon as the circle was back up, her body was turned, straightened, and placed at the center as we see her now, but I never touched her. And before you try to kill me again"—he glared at Samir with courage I had no idea he possessed—"I'm one hundred percent sure there is nothing else there with her. It was the magic of the circle that did it…I think." The witch scratched at his forehead and turned the washed-out green eyes on me, hopelessness clear in them.

My mind was reeling trying to come up with answers I had no way of knowing. On principle, I stayed away from the witches while I was under the roof of the Council. Magic was a foreign concept to me. *'But not to Alice.'* A tiny, barely audible whisper spoke in the back of my mind.

How much did they know about my friend? Was Samir aware she is the *Mmico* they are waiting for their prophecy? I had a suspicion Dominic suspected there was something special about our human friend, plus he started caring for her much to his displeasure. So, I was not worried that he may see her as a tool to be used. Rowen and the demons were a wild card. I had to be careful what I said in front of them.

Echo saved me from guessing.

"How very peculiar." The male demon inched closer to the circle while giving Dominic a wide berth, side-eyeing him warily. "The whole gadget's usage—candles, crystals and herbs—is different, but this is how we normally heal if we are gravely injured. In a circle though, because we are in our most vulnerable state."

"Shut up, Chester." Echo hissed at him, balling her hands into fists at her sides. I had no doubt she was imagining she was holding Chester's throat. "What is the matter with you telling our weaknesses, you idiot."

"Can you stop talking to me like I'm some simpleton?" Lifting to his full height, he glowered at the much shorter demon. "Were you not present in that foyer when we fought? We don't need to be at our weakest for them to kill us." Waving a hand frantically in the direction of Alice, he shook his head. "Maybe if we help with this one, they'll return the favor." After a long staring match with Echo, he blew out a heavy sigh muttering under his breath. "If we stay alive long enough."

They continued bickering amongst each other, but a brand-new hope bloomed in my chest. Digging my nails into Dominic's forearm, which I hadn't noticed I was still clinging to, I turned us to Rowen, urgency making me sound breathless and meek.

"Rowen, when did this happen?" Waiting for his answer, I held my breath.

A line formed between the eyebrows on the witch's face, and a weird sequence of glowing lights passed over the sigils there. "I'm sorry, what?"

"When did you reopen the circle and have Alice placed like this in it?" My voice broke a few times, but I managed to get the words out.

"Umm…" Rowen's eyes darted around the room as he attempted to remember and finally, he limply shrugged one shoulder. "About twenty? Maybe thirty minutes ago." After blowing out a long breath, his eyes lit up. "Around the time I heard your voice in the foyer. I'm sure of it because that's why Alice wanted to break the circle so she could come show you she's better."

"I do not understand." Annoyed for being ignored, Samir rose from his crouch. "Someone better explain what is going on."

"Do you trust me?" Continuing to ignore the arrogant Atua, I turned to face Dominic.

"Yes." There was no hesitation, no doubt or second guessing. Only firm confidence and belief in me shone through those emerald eyes as they watched me steadily.

Warmth spread through my chest, thawing the frost crusting my heart after the bloodbaths I left all over Chicago. On a whim, I popped up on my tiptoes and pressed my lips on his, hoping it relayed all my gratitude for his support. I had to fix all the hurt I'd caused him since we met, but it was neither the time nor the place.

Strong arms wrapped around my back, pressing me to his chest as if he were too afraid I might disappear if he didn't hold me hard enough. The desperation I felt in his touch broke me anew, and I stood there a bit longer, offering the intimacy he needed and deserved.

"I will explain everything later," I told him a little breathlessly after we broke the kiss. "I need to speak to Echo and Chester alone, in this room." I pointedly turned my eyes to Samir and Rowen too.

Samir had his mouth open to start arguing when Rowen, for the first time, acted out of character and grabbed him by the shoulders. The Atua was taken by surprise hard enough that he was out the door gaping like a fish at the witch before his brain got online again and he started shouting and threatening. Dominic was already closing the door behind him at that point so I knew he would keep them out.

My heart skipped a beat when he gave me a quick wink before the lock clicked shut.

"Well?" Chester asked warily. "Talk about what?"

"How long do you guys heal when you are in a sleep like this?" I cut to the chase, pointing at Alice.

"From a few hours to a few days, depending on the injury." Echo frowned, probably wondering if I'd lost my mind.

"Well, we need to figure out how to keep Samir and Rowen out of this room by then." Slapping my hands on my hips, I looked around the room, hoping to find...what? An armoire that would block the door?

"Brooklyn!" Samir's voice came through the wooden door loud and clear. "Open this door immediately!"

Chester was watching me too thoughtfully for my liking, but finally he said what I needed to hear. "Do you really want to keep them out of this room?"

"Yes."

"Not even a witch can break demon magic." With a gloating grin, he tugged the sleeves of his ripped shirt in places and raised his hands toward the door. After a second, Echo joined him, the same troublesome smile on her lips.

Red glowing lights surrounded the door and the frame holding it.

"Brooklyn!" Samir's roar was followed by Dominic's guffaw.

Despite the situation, I had to smile and shake my head.

Chapter Eleven

DOMINIC

She accepted our bond.

If anyone told me that I would fear a tiny female, an Atua at that, more than anything in my entire existence, I would've laughed in their face. Hells, I had laughed in the face of death more times than I could count, but a cold sweat covered me, and numbness spread through me just thinking about Brooklyn walking away from our bond.

But she didn't.

A stupid smile stretched my mouth so wide my face hurt.

While Samir was having a tantrum, threatening every-one, mostly Rowen to open the door so he could see what they were doing with the human, I grinned at him like a fool, and arms folded over my chest, I leaned back on the door which was now glowing red.

Brooklyn called me mate, convinced my animal to shift forms with me, and not even an hour later looked at me with her soul shining through her gaze and asked me to trust her. I had no idea what they were doing inside that room, but I trusted my mate. She would never harm Alice, unlike me. And she trusted those demons to bring them to our hiding place, so I had every intention to keep my word.

No one was walking in through the door.

Agonizing pain forked all over my back and shoulders the moment my body touched the wood. Whatever magic they used to make it glow red latched onto my body, keeping me glued to the door while it stabbed through every nerve ending I had until I couldn't even scream from the intensity of it. All I could do was keep my eyes tightly squeezed shut and my mouth wide open in a silent scream.

A slight relief came from in front of me. Like pouring cold water over a burn to soothe the ache for a second, but it was gone before I could take a breath. It repeated a couple of times, and each time I thought I heard Rowen mutter something angrily, but I couldn't be sure. Trains were thudding between my ears while my beast kept thrashing in hopes to force me to shift.

Fat chance I was going to let that happen.

I was ready to give Brooklyn the time she needed even if it cost me my life.

Something hit me from the side, but it bounced off without pushing me too much aside to have to abandon my post. Although I wanted to see what or who it was, I couldn't open my eyes. Just like my teeth, my eyelids were practically glued together from the agony passing through me in waves. Secretly, I hoped it was Samir so that I could finally have a reason to knock him on his pompous ass.

Suddenly, I was hit so hard, my body went flying halfway down the hallway, slamming into one of the random plaster torsos the ancient Atua was collecting as if they were some precious possessions and not a creepy obsession with dead people. The disturbing decoration shattered into small parts which sprayed everywhere. Samir's colorful description of how he felt about it penetrated through the fog in my mind, and I wished I could continue to be in the horrible pain just so I didn't have to listen to him.

"The three of you open this gods forsaken door or I will bring the roof down over your heads, Brooklyn!" He shook with rage as he turned his glare to the still glowing door.

I guess cursing me out and telling me where he hoped an ogre would stick his thick dangling appendage left him out of steam with threats for me; so, he focused again on my mate. I chuckled through my misery. It pleased me to no end to see him this pissed.

Rowen, who was kneeling next to me and checking if I was about to keel over, frowned with displeasure. "I fail to find humor in any of this," he mumbled angrily under his breath. I noticed a bruise blooming on the side of his head, his temple turning bluish, telling me he was the first one who tried to move me from the door. A few more snorts and chuckles escaped me. "Did you hit your head or did the demon magic fry your brain? None of this is funny, Dominic. We are harboring demons now. What is next? The cursed Fae?"

"Ah! That's what that was." On a groan, I rolled to my side, hoping to sit up. The world tilted around me, and I plopped back down with a hiss. "Demon magic is no joke, I agree."

"Tricksters, Dominic," Rowen spat while Samir continued having a one-sided argument with the door. "They're all charlatans and frauds."

"Who?" I squinted at him. "The demons?"

"What? Stop shouting, they could hear you." The witch reeled back as if I had just slapped him. "The Fae. Is anyone even listening to me?"

"Someone must've cursed me to deal with you and Captain Droopy Drawers over there. It's the only explanation for my life right now." Grinding my teeth, I pushed off the floor and managed to get on my knees without melting from the killer glance the ancient Atua threw my way. Breathing through the nausea was harder with Samir raging like a toddler having a tantrum a few feet from me. "Samir?"

"How dare you lock me out of my own rooms." The Atua ignored me and shook his fist at Brooklyn who could not see him or his red face. "Gods damn demons! Do you know who I am?"

"Samir!" Holding myself up with a hand on the wall, I rose to my shaking feet while Rowen fretted around me like a mother hen. "Damn, that pain did a number on me. I'll tell you who you are, Samir. If you didn't flap your gums so much that I can see all those teeth, I would've guessed you are an asshole."

"I can endure many things, shifter." Whirling on me, Samir squared his shoulders and yanked on his button-down to straighten the nonexistent wrinkles. "Your childish insults, however, are not one of them. Not today." Leaning forward, he bared his fangs in my face on a hiss. "You think this is some philanthropic gesture from the demons? If one hair goes missing on that human's head, I will gorge on your blood. On all of your bloods."

"Do you hear yourself?" Leaning a shoulder on the wall to hold myself up, I scrubbed a hand over my face. "That's Brooklyn inside with Alice. Can you be honest with yourself, not me, and tell me if you truly believe my mate will hurt her best friend? She nearly ripped my head off for the human. At this point, I wish the demons do try something so she can kill them both and be done with it."

"Messing with demons never ends well." Rowen shuddered, his mouth twisting in disgust. "They are vile creatures."

"Some may say the same of your kind, too, Witch." Samir sniffed haughtily at the male, looking down his nose at him. "I will mess with whomever well I please."

The whole situation was getting out of hand, and I was left with little to no patience. My mate was counting on me to have her back, and by all the gods I was going to have it.

"What did you do to Alice, Rowen?" As soon as the words were out of my mouth I realized my mistake.

While angry to be locked out of the room, Samir totally forgot the reason it happened. Now that I reminded him, he turned all that fury on the witch and before I could stop him, he picked up the shorter male and threw him all the way to the end of the hallway. Rowen flew head over ass with a high-pitched shriek before colliding with the wall and part of the elaborate window frame.

"This is all your fault," Samir thundered and bolted after him.

I started to move in their direction as well, to separate them or get a few punches in to relieve my frustration with both of them, but I paused. Was it really a bad thing for the two of them to fight? As long as I kept an eye on them and made sure the witch did not die, a few bruises might do them both some good.

"I've had enough of you bullying me, Samir." Rowen fought, kicked, and punched to untangle himself from the thick velvet drapes where he ended up rolling into, his voice muffled from the fabric. "I am no longer your subordinate and it's time for you to learn that I have kept my head down only because I chose to."

"Oh, shit," I said on a breath when the witch finally stepped out of the long drapes.

The robes had ripped down on one side, exposing a naked upper body that was not as bony as I expected it to be. Rounded, well-formed muscles twitched as he rolled his shoulders and the visible sigils were glowing so bright it was almost difficult to look at him.

"You will always be lesser." With a menacing grin, Samir gloated at the witch. "You were born to serve me."

It happened too fast to see exactly what Rowen did, but one moment Samir was grinning like a villain, the next bright golden light burst between the witch's hands in a steady stream and jabbed him in the center of his chest. A pain filled shout came from the Atua like I'd never heard before, and his body was flung back at the wall behind him. It hit with a tooth shattering crunch, and he ended up on the floor with his extremities at awkward angles.

Seeing the ancient Atua in a heap on the floor took the wind out of Rowen's sails.

"What did I do?" he whispered, horrified at what he was looking at.

I could lie and say it was not a good sight, but I was usually honest with myself for the most part. It felt damn good to see that arrogant prick sprawled like a broken puppet on the Persian runner.

"I'll be damned, Rowen." Chuckling low, I shook my head, but the humor died on my tongue when the male turned guilt-ridden eyes on me. "I didn't think you had it in you." Shrugging an unapologetic shoulder, I inched closer and kicked Samir with the tip of my boot to check if he was awake.

"I shouldn't have done that." Self-consciously he tugged on the ripped part of his robe. "And for the record, I only tried to help Alice like she was one of my kind because it felt like the right thing to do. The opportunity presented itself, and I took it. It worked." The guilt was replaced with defiance when he jutted a stubborn jaw at that. "For the most part it worked, anyway. I don't understand what happened there at the end."

Just like Samir, I wanted to grab him by the neck and squeeze until he stopped moving, but the logical part of my brain told me that he at least tried to do something. Everything else the rest of us attempted didn't cut it. Alice was slowly slipping through our fingers, and it was my fault. I placed her in harm's way regardless of what way I justified my actions. Instead of yelling at Rowen, I should've thanked him.

The fact that Brooklyn looked very hopeful when she asked me to keep the two males out of the room was a plus in the witch's favor of course.

"Thank you for trying," I decided to tell him.

"Huh?" His face scrunched up in confusion as he looked up at me. "You are not going to try and kill me like this one?" his hand flopped in the direction of the now twitching heap that was Samir.

I snorted and Rowen's lips twitched.

"Nah. We are good." I slapped his shoulder, and he stumbled away a few steps before he caught himself. "Besides, we have all the time in the world for Samir to come about and try to kill you again. It'll be like watching one of those action movies that Alice likes."

When Rowen gave me a mean glare I couldn't help it.

I threw my head back and laughed.

"I'm going to gut you, Witch," came a hiss from the floor.

"And it starts." I grinned like a fiend at Rowen.

Chapter Twelve

BROOKLYN

I wondered if anyone noticed that there was a spiderweb stretching from one corner of the room to the dangling light in the center of it. Tucking my knees closer to my chest and wrapping my arms around them, I continued to observe it, picturing Samir's face if he ever saw it. I had no doubt he would be horrified. I always thought there was some magic placed in and around the structure that kept the mansion always clean.

I guess I was wrong.

The spider was nowhere to be seen I noticed, nor were there any flies or bugs wrapped up in the web. Just a beautiful interwoven string crossing and twisting from one end to the other. It shimmered in places where the light hit it at the right angle, as well. Quite fascinating really, and much better to occupy my thoughts than stressing about... everything.

"Do you want to talk about it?" Chester glanced at me through his lashes from across the room where he was watching something through the window. "You know, whatever made you look all sad and…that." Turning to face me, he waved a hand in my direction, encompassing my pitiful state where I was hugging my knees on the floor.

"Better yet"—Echo squat-walked a few feet around the circle where Alice was still sleeping, tilting her head this way and that as if she'd get a different view from the one, we'd all been staring at for the last few hours—"want to share why the human is acting like she is a demon? Because she's not a demon, right?"

"I don't know how to do magic." Going for nonchalant and ignoring her last question, I shrugged an unconcerned shoulder, although my heart was drumming in my throat. "How would I know what the witch did? I would make a deal with the devil himself if it would help save my friend. You said she's healing. That's all I needed to hear." My finger twitched toward Alice like Echo had no idea who I was referring to. "I asked Dominic to keep everyone out of here so we can give her enough time."

"The witch can do demon magic?" Echo dramatically rolled her neck to spear me with a well-practiced dubious expression. If there was one thing I noticed about these two demons, they had the penchant for dramatics and hullabaloo.

"How would I know what the witch can do, Echo? You said it'll take time." I reminded her, using her comments to cover my own butt. "Didn't she say that, Chester?"

"Oh, hells, no." The demon flopped his hands around as if he was attacked by a cloud of bees. "Don't drag me into your…whatever this is. I dislike those two that tried to kill us as soon as we entered this house, so I placed a seal on the door so they can't come in." Sucking in a loud, long breath he smoothed a hand over his chest with a smirk. "To piss them off. On purpose. I'm not on your side."

"The two of you attacked them first," I reminded him.

"I don't know when it was the last time you checked with the Syndicate, Girl." He cocked his hip and slapped a hand on it. "That schmuck out there that just stopped shrieking like a banshee." Pausing for a dramatic effect and so that he could stare me down until I was the first one to blink, he nodded as if I confirmed his superior status. "That's the Syndicate. A wolf can dress in sheep's clothing, he is still a gods damn wolf."

"I mean, I see your point." I couldn't argue with his logic, and I took responsibility for my actions. I should've warned them. "He is not Syndicate though. He betrayed the Council to protect me. I owe him a benefit of a doubt at least."

"You do not trust him fully?" Echo dropped her pretenses, her tone earnest and her eyes unguarded.

"No," I answered her honestly. "He has proven time and again that I should, yet I can't bring myself to fully remove my doubt. There is just something…" my words cut off when I realized I said too much.

Not fully trusting Samir had more to do with protecting Alice than whether or not he harbored feelings for his buddies on the Council. But I couldn't tell the demons that because I learned a lesson. As my human friend loved reminding me, we show our dirty laundry only to those we trust.

"I like her." Chester announced, like that was the most important thing in the situation we found ourselves in.

"Shut it, Chip. Nobody asked you." The female hissed at him playfully. "I like her too, though. She has no deceit about her. I'm glad we decided to approach her."

"Your brothers would disagree." I mumbled under my

breath, still feeling awkward about the whole you-killed-my-brothers-but-we-can-still-be-friends thing.

"Sorry, what?" Echo frowned, leaning forward to hear me better the second time.

So not happening.

"Nothing. I said I'm glad you agreed to approach me." How was that for no deceit about me? Alice would've been very proud of me for keeping a straight face. "I know that we are somewhat of an unorthodox group, but we make it work. And just to make it clear, you can count on any of us to have your back as long as you don't betray us. Because if you do, and I'm not killed"—locking gazes with Echo and then Chester for long enough that they understood the weight of my words, I spoke clear and concise so they couldn't say later we had a misunderstanding—"there is no place you can hide where I will not find you. And killing you will be last on the list of things I will do to you before I end your life."

Chester swallowed loudly and shivered, while Echo, still squatting near the circle, watched me with an interest I couldn't decipher. It may not have been a good way of starting an alliance, yet I did not regret a word I said.

"Brooklyn is never one to waste words." The slurring came from the center of the circle, and my head snapped toward Alice who was grinning sleepily at me. "The girl has no dexterity to save her life. She just slaps it out there," she told the demons on a yawn. I watched her dumbly as she slowly pushed herself up to sit and adjusted the glasses upon her nose with her forefinger. "Kinda like what she did now when she threatened you."

"How do you feel?" I crawled on hands and knees to get closer to where she was in the room from my perch in front of the sealed door. Samir's threats and shouting might've ended after all the crashing noises we heard a couple of hours ago, but I didn't trust the male not to try something when we least expected it.

My hand started lifting so I could reach for Alice, but I remembered the protection of the circle, so I froze halfway. "Is this thing going to zap me if I try and touch it?" My question was directed at the demons, but it was Alice who answered.

"No. The protection is gone." She frowned first at the salt used to draw the circle then at me. "Why do I know that?" Confusion twisted her features. "Better yet, how do I know that?"

"Rowen has a lot of explaining to do." I rushed to cut off whatever else she was going to say.

When she inhaled—I assumed to ask why Rowen had to explain anything—I continued talking while giving her a pointed glare to keep her questions to herself for now. "Most important right now is that you are feeling better. You are feeling better, aren't you, Alice?"

"I feel great." As if surprised by her own admission, she lifted her arms to examine them and turned this way and that to check her legs and the rest of her body. "I feel like I have slept for a month. Brooklyn, I never feel this good. Oh my God!"

Excitedly, she turned on her knees and yanked on the sleeve of her shirt to expose her elbow. Swiping her hair away from her face, she tried to get a good look at it, bending her arm at very awkward and painful looking angles. The entire time she kept repeating 'oh. my God.'

"What is it?" I slid close to her, breaking the line of the circle with my knees.

The demons stayed silent, but Echo moved near my friend as well from her other side. We all stared at absolutely nothing while Alice fretted excitedly. Going as far as to crane her neck and attempt to kiss her elbow.

She was so strange sometimes.

"Nothing!" she squealed with exhilaration and jabbed her elbow in my face, stopping a hair before hitting my nose. "It's absolutely nothing, Brooklyn! It's wonderful."

"I don't normally interact with humans much." Echo's face was too large when she spoke since she leaned in to see what Alice was showing me, placing both of us almost nose to nose. My eyes almost crossed so I could see her. "Are they all like this one?"

"What's that supposed to mean?" Alice leaned in too, as close as keeping her elbow pointed at my face would allow her. "And what are you?" She lifted an eyebrow at Echo.

"Slow," the demon female told me since I didn't answer her question.

"Who are you calling slow?" Alice sharply dropped her elbow down, making me jerk back so she didn't break my nose. "Who is this mean person, Brooklyn. If she's a friend of yours, let me tell you, you need new friends." Lips pursed, she jutted her chin out to stare down Echo. "Don't you worry though, you have me. You don't need the meanie."

My mouth opened, but I had no chance to say a word.

"You are the one acting like you've never known that you have an elbow." Echo jabbed a finger at my friend. "How do you not know what body parts you have? I've seen enough of your kind to know you are not a youngling. That makes you slow."

"It makes me happy that the tennis elbow which has been bothering me for a few years is gone." Alice was practically vibrating from anger as she glared at the demon.

"You had two elbows?" With a line cutting a groove

between her eyebrows, Echo looked from me to Alice, horrified.

Groaning, Alice placed her face in both hands and muttered unintelligible words through her fingers. My mind was reeling that she was feeling well enough to be her normal self and voice her opinion on things that bothered her. In this case, Echo insulting her, although I was sure the female demon didn't mean to do it. I'd insulted Alice many times since we'd met, but she always looked through my shortcomings and continued to be my friend. Which told me I was a horrible one for not defending her.

"I had tendonitis, thank you very much." My friend told Echo. "It's an inflammation and it hurts like a bitch. But now it's gone along with a scar I had from that one time I fell off my bike and scraped the shit out of my skin there." Giggling, she shook her head and had to adjust her glasses again. "My mom was so angry. Oh boy, my poor dad had to sleep in the RV a few days because of it. Look." She jabbed the elbow in Echo's face, still snorting at the memory she freely shared with us, unaware of how precious her human life was compared to the nightmares we lived. "No scar, no pain, nothing. I feel like a whole human being for the first time in my life."

"I like the human, too," Chester decided loudly, and the three of us jumped from the sound of his voice. We'd forgotten he was there. "And here we are. No one cares if I'm here or not. Might as well go out and let the Syndicate kill me. No one will care if I die."

"Stop being a drama queen, Chip." Echo's mouth turned into a squiggly line from his theatrics. "You are missing the most important thing here."

"Thank you." Alice beamed at Chester and stuck her tongue out at Echo.

"I still want to know why the human healed like a demon." Echo turned those shimmering eyes on me.

"Hey." Alice surged up on her knees and stabbed her finger at the female demon. "Stop with the insults. First slow, now demon. I don't point out that your nose is too long or that you have no tits." Sniffing with indignation, she glared at Echo whose jaw dropped at the outburst. "What? You didn't know you had no boobs? Look at them. They're like sunny side up eggs. Just nipples."

You could hear a needle drop, and all I could hear was the jackhammering of my heart in my ears.

Chester burst out laughing. "Well, damnnnn."

Chapter Thirteen

ALICE

A giggle burst out of me when the dude standing by the window started laughing. His joy was contagious, and soon I was chortling along with him, with tears streaming down my face. If I stopped for a moment and thought about it, I would've apologized to the girl whose jaw continued to sweep the floor.

It was mean, what I said to her.

She started it first though. It was childish to laugh triumphantly, but for the moment it made me forget about the emptiness, pain and numbness I had felt for a long time. Just because I had no idea how much time had passed since the night Brooklyn attacked me, it made no difference to the fear clinging to every fiber of my being. Not that it was her fault, or that I would ever blame her for it. All I could remember was one second, I was just standing there, and the next Brooklyn was too close and her teeth were pressing on my neck.

And the cold.

A brain-numbing chill that penetrated the bone marrow.

There was so much blood; I had no idea I had that much liquid inside of me. We all heard how much a human body could hold, but it was a lot different to see it with your very own eyes. Especially if it was spraying and pumping from your throat.

Oh, God, I was so cold.

The adrenaline was pumping through me while we were executing our plan, but the moment my life trickled down the front of me, the chill spread from my toes up toward the crown of my head like frost forming on windows in the middle of winter. I could still feel it biting at me from the inside, but for the sake of my friend, I kept the smile stretching my face while looking at her.

"She is not a demon." Brooklyn narrowed her eyes at the girl sitting on the floor with us, ready as always to start ripping heads off to protect me. "Alice, this is Echo and Chester." My friend did the introductions and I nodded at the two people. "They are the demons."

Smiling still, my gaze jumped from the guy to the girl a few more times before Brooklyn's last words penetrated my brain. When they finally did, I was on my feet and running for the door.

"Let's go, girl." Shouting and glancing over my shoulder to make sure Brooklyn was right behind me, I almost head-butted the wall when I saw her holding her forehead like I was giving her a headache. Thanks to my faster than ever reflexes, I didn't touch anywhere near the red glow on and around the door. Whatever they did to heal me worked wonders. I felt great and had a lot more strength than I remembered. "Don't look at their eyes! Let's go, let's go.

The door is compromised. We can use the window, or just bust through a wall. I'm sure you'll be fine."

"Why are you not supposed to look at our eyes?" Echo was gazing up at me from where she was folded on the floor in puzzlement, and I jerked my gaze away from her when I realized I was not following my own advice.

"You've been looking at our eyes since you woke up." Chester pointed out dryly at the same time.

"I asked them to come here, Alice." Brooklyn told me on a sigh. "They won't hurt you."

"That's exactly what you'd say if you were possessed. Or blackmailed." I shook my head at her. Couldn't she see what was going on? "Hello. Use your brain."

"We are not ghosts." I was shocked dust was not coming out of the strange woman's mouth from how dry her tone was. Stubbornly, I kept my eyes glued on Brooklyn and ignored her existence while trying hard not to hyperventilate. "We can't possess humans."

"Right, and I'm a blonde bombshell that just signed a contract with Victoria's Secret." Snorting, I inched closer to the opposite wall, pushing my glasses up my nose since they annoyingly continued to slip down, my eyes darting around the room in case more of them popped up out of nowhere. I've seen enough movies to know demons can just appear out of nowhere. They must've drugged Brooklyn or blackmailed her to stay docile while these two were roaming around our place, I was sure of it.

"Where are Dominic, Samir and Rowen?" Looking pointedly at my friend, I let her see my eyebrows crawling all the way up to my hairline, silently telling her *'Wake up girl, they are prepping us like freshly made shish kebabs ready to be roasted.'* "Where is my dog?"

"He's a wolf, Alice, not a dog, and I'm sure Samir

locked him up in one of the rooms because it annoyed him. Otherwise, the males are outside the door." In a smooth move, Brooklyn was on her feet dusting off the herbs from her pants with a look of distaste. "I messed up things with Dominic, but he still does anything I ask of him. I will need your help to fix that. Anyway, we needed time for you to heal without interference, and I asked him to keep the witch and Samir out."

"The demons are doctors?" My heartbeat just started to slow down because that would make sense why she wasn't worried about them while the Syndicate, plus everyone and their brothers, were trying to kill us.

"What?" Brooklyn barked out a laugh and glanced at me sideways. "No. They're not doctors. A funny story really. They are my kidnapers actually…"

"I knew it!" Frantically spinning in a circle, I snatched the first thing I could see that could be used as a weapon.

The elaborately painted vase full of wildflowers was heavier than I anticipated, and water sloshed all over my hand, the long t-shirt someone dressed me in, as well as the floor when it tilted harshly, and I came dangerously close to dropping it but managed to grab it and hug it to my chest. "Step away from them, Brooklyn. Like hell I will let them do something to you after everything we went through to get you back." Without thinking how wise it was, I rushed back to my friend, stepped in front of her, and jabbed the vase at the still-sitting-on-the-floor demon.

"Stay back, or I'll cut you." Snarling at her would've been more intimidating if my glasses didn't drop to one side and hang sideways on my face, but I didn't care. Also, a pool of water was forming at my feet, and flowers were dropping one by one in it. That totally rained on my parade.

"Fascinating." The woman demon craned her neck to look at the dude who was watching us with an unnaturally wide grin on his face from next to the window. "The human is trying to protect one of us. It's beautiful to watch."

"Actually, I'm not protecting anything when it comes to the rest of you. I will gut you. I'm protecting my friend. Get out!" The vase was much lighter without the water and blooms, so I brandished it in the demon's face like a baseball bat. "Dear Father in Heaven, protect us in these times."

"Alice? What are you doing?" Brooklyn tried to walk around me, but I reached back and made sure she stayed there. Maybe she was still vulnerable to things after dealing with the tainted blood in her system. I didn't know if she could stand being around demons. Better safe than sorry, I continued praying.

"I know I'm not always the most faithful, but I'll do better, I promise. For now, I love you and I pray that you will smite these demons, burn their soulless corpses, and cast them to the armpits of hell." My prayer was getting louder as I spoke, the strength of my need to save my best friend from these creatures giving it more passion than anything else in my life. "Amen."

Silence charged with expectation stretched around us so thick you could cut it with a knife. It reminded me of the time the Guardians attacked us in my father's safe house and the magic glued the breadknife to my hand. How I wished I had it now so that if the two demons attacked, I could slice them up.

Gathering as much strength as I could, I made myself lock eyes with the woman still sitting on the floor. Silver, like lightning, shimmered over her irises, and goosebumps popped up all over my arms. It really made me angry that she smiled sweetly when I couldn't resist it and had to fix the glasses so they weren't dangling from the side of my face.

"Were you praying to your God to kill us?" the dude by the window asked incredulously.

"If he doesn't succeed, I'm pretty sure I can get the shifter and the vamp who live in this house to do it." Baring my teeth at his shocked face, I waved the vase at the woman with silver eyes. "Open the door so we can leave."

"Alice."

"Don't Alice me, Brooklyn, I got this, don't worry. No one is going to be kidnaping you or me." Narrowing my eyes at both demons, I repeated myself. "Remove whatever magic you placed on that door right now. I won't ask you again."

"We will, of course." The female demon slowly and carefully rose to her feet, which placed her roughly around my height. "We only placed it because Brooklyn asked. But out of curiosity…" Cocking her head to the side she seemed intrigued by the situation. Her braid swung like a rope over her shoulder and dangled backward and forward innocently for a long moment. "What do you think you can do if we don't do what you demand?"

"Me?" I laughed humorlessly at her. Fatigue started to creep up and I found it difficult to hold the vase between us, but I had to hold on for just a bit longer. "I won't do anything." My smile was probably more a grimace than an expression of happiness. "But he will."

"Who?" the woman frowned at me.

"My friends, of course." Adrenaline shot through me as I opened my mouth and screamed from the top of my lungs, making Brooklyn grab her ears and duck her head from the high-pitched sound. "Dominic! Samir! Help!"

The magic around the door was glowing red undisturbed when the walls came crashing down around it and a pissed off shifter and vamp stood shoulder to shoulder, panting with rage in the middle of the dust cloud.

My lips twitched when I heard Brooklyn whisper from behind me. "Oh, shit."

I was so totally going to save her this time, again.

Chapter Fourteen

BROOKLYN

"Everyone stop!" The extra punch from my curse assured my wishes were followed, leaving everyone in peculiar states.

Samir was halfway to Echo, teeth bared and fingers clawed, ready to tear her apart. There was murder written in his furious eyes. Dominic had his full attention focused on Chester after his gaze skipped all over me from head to toe checking for injuries, and he saw Alice was unharmed standing in front of me with that ridiculous vase. Rowen was peeking out from behind them, eyes wide and sigils lit up in a rapid pattern. Plaster and white dust covered all of them and the cloud was spreading around to fill the room.

"We will be fine now, don't worry." Alice turned her head to look at me over her shoulder. "No one is kidnaping my bestie."

"We were fine before, as well." There was a pounding headache forming right above the right side of my cheekbone, sending waves of nausea through me, making me unsteady on my feet. "Everyone in this house is here because we are trying to help you, Alice. Please put the vase down and lie down until we are sure you are fully healed."

After a long moment and a nod from Dominic, she sheepishly cringed and gingerly placed the vase at her feet in the pool of water. I meant to do the right thing for her by bringing the demons to help her, but, yet again, I managed to make a mess out of things.

I was drained.

Mentally and emotionally.

To prove that fact, my curse couldn't hold the males much longer and they reanimated again. Thankfully, the promise of being told what to do again did its trick, and no one attacked anyone. However, there was a ton of glaring between all of them.

Scratching and soft whimpering reached my ears, coming from somewhere in the hallway, and I stabbed Samir with a pointed glare. He knew why I was sending him death threats through my gaze because all of us could hear the wolf attempting to get out of whatever room he was locked in. All of us but Alice.

"What's that noise?" My human friend pushed her glasses up her nose with a forefinger and glanced from Dominic to me. "Can you hear it?"

It appeared that I was wrong. Watching her tilt her head this way and that, I couldn't help but wonder what other changes have occurred in her thanks to our meddling in her life. Afraid she was losing too much blood that cursed night, Samir and I both gave her some of ours in hopes to help with healing.

It didn't.

When that didn't work, Dominic tried, too, thinking that the accelerated healing of his shifter ability was a closer match to humans than ours. Time proved him wrong as well. Nothing changed apart from Rowen's ability to feed her potions that smelled vile but kept her afloat. Nothing healed her, but it kept her alive.

Until I brought the demons right at the time the witch decided to experiment with my friend. Now she could hear sounds that no human ever could. Everyone in the room was ignoring Alice's strange behavior. All of them were looking at me with accusatory eyes, like I knew something they didn't and was refusing to share.

I did, of course.

I just had no intention to share, yet.

Not until I knew which one of them I could trust.

"I had to place the wolf away from you so I could try to do the spell, Alice." Rowen stepped through the large hole in the wall warily glancing at the red glowing door. "He wouldn't let me move you from the bed, so I took a steak from the fridge and lured him to the end of the hallway."

"You fed that mongrel my steak?" Dominic glowered at the witch.

"I didn't see you coming up with new ideas of what to do. I'll replace your steak." Rowen shuffled his feet faster when a low growl started in Dominic's throat. "Besides. That wolf was starving. He was dripping saliva all down the hall. When was the last time anyone fed him?"

He wasn't fully finished talking when Alice bolted out of the room, jumping like a gazelle through the hole, the long t-shirt bunched up in both hands and her skinny legs barely missing the sharp edges. She muttered something about her soul burning in hell and that was why the demons came to get her. I flinched when the crashing noise came a moment later. My friend was throwing something at the door holding her pet as she called him.

"Everyone needs to stop destroying my property." Samir

huffed and spun on his heel, speed-walked after Alice. "I will be discussing all of this with you later, Brooklyn," he threw over his shoulder as his head disappeared from view.

"I'm sure you will." My grousing made Dominic's full lips curl slightly at the corners, and like a lovesick fool, I smiled shyly at him.

Until Echo cleared her throat.

I frowned at the shifter then for making me lose focus of the people in the room.

"Not that this is any of my business, but I still would like to know why a witch was healing a human in a magic circle and that human was displaying demon attributes." Echo folded her arms across her chest and widened her stance like a Guardian.

I disliked that stance so much that it took effort not to start another squabble with everyone getting involved. Time was slipping away, however, and we needed to get some things out of the way before we could focus on more important things.

Like the Syndicate.

"I thought your presence did something that caused that." Ignorance was my best friend at the time when I had to keep Alice's secret a little bit longer, and I hoped Dominic would just play along with it. "Could it be that your presence somehow interfered with the magic Rowen was using?" Glancing between them, I shrugged. "I know nothing about witch magic or demon magic for that matter. I just assumed…"

"I've never heard of anything like it." Rowen scratched at his head while thoughtfully watching the two demons. "I'd been told the two cancel each other out, which is why they can place wards we can't breach and the other way around."

The three of them were nodding in unison, agreeing with the facts Rowen shared, and with that, destroying the sham I was waving to protect my friend. Desperately, I turned to my mate and begged him with my eyes to help.

"If that was true, demons would've stormed the base where the Syndicate operates from long ago. Witch magic is the only thing keeping them safe there. They must interact somehow; you just might not know it," Dominic reasoned as he moved closer to me so we represented a unified front.

It warmed my insides, and I leaned slightly into him.

"They do storm that dreadful place on a regular basis, but the Atua have been using that weakness to their advantage. Guardians are tripled in the regular breach spots to capture them," Rowen explained through clenched teeth, his right-hand twisting in the fabric of his robes. "Demons aren't known for playing well with others, or each other, they never have the numbers to achieve anything with those attacks."

"He speaks the truth." Chester chirped from his place by the window. "Being unable to agree on things has been our downfall. Which is why despite the survival odds, we came to you." His chin jutted out, pointing at me.

"Brooklyn is a very reasonable female." Dominic puffed up his chest, and I gaped at him. "If you have information worthy of notice, she would hear you out at any time."

Rowen was eagerly nodding his head, his face lit with excitement to not be put on the spot anymore. "Oh, yes. She is somewhat of a celebrity in the supernatural world. She took on the Syndicate head on and she's winning."

"Have you met her?" Echo stabbed a finger at me all wide-eyed. "Go tell that to two of my brothers. Oh wait, you can't. They're dead because she killed them."

"You said you weren't holding a grudge for it, but I see

your point," I told her earnestly and blew out a large amount of air until I got lightheaded. "We should go somewhere else to talk. I don't know about the rest of you, but I like to surprise my lungs with fresh air on occasion when I'm not locked up in a cage."

"I have no doubt the rest of you are hungry." Rowen got animated flipping around with a flourish and waving at us to follow him. I had never seen him that cheerful. He probably hated being the center of attention as much as I did. "I'm famished and Samir had a lot of food delivered earlier in the day. You know, in case the human woke up and needed nourishment."

"The rest of you don't?" Echo asked but followed right behind the witch. "Or is he keeping you on a diet?"

Chester snorted but stayed where he was, in his favorite place by the window. "We don't necessarily need to eat."

"No, but it's delicious when we do." She glanced back at him, grinning.

"You are not coming?" I expected him to be the first to rush after Rowen who was standing in the hallway and watching us through the hole while Echo was jumping through the debris to join him, but the male just stood there, one shoulder propped on the wall and his face half toward us half facing the window.

"I'd like to stay here a little longer if you don't mind." Both his eyebrows pulled over his eyes, and he leaned closer to the window. "There is just something nagging me about that far left area of the property and I want to make sure it's just my imagination and not something serious before I join you."

"You think there is someone there?" I was walking away with Dominic but that made me pause. Intrigued, I moved back next to him and tried to follow his line of sight.

"I'm not sure," the demon mumbled, his breath fogging the glass. His nose was slightly pressing on the window while he struggled to understand what it was that bothered him. "A few times I thought I saw something move but after staring for a long time it appeared to be no..."

"There." Dominic reached over my shoulder and pointed right at a silhouette that passed from one tall bush to the next in the manicured lawn Samir took pride in. "Samir, bring Alice here immediately. We have a problem."

He didn't need to shout, because the next second, we heard thudding footsteps coming down the hall and Samir popped in through the hole carrying an outraged Alice over his shoulder. The wolf throttled alongside them and gazed suspiciously at all of us, including me. When our gazes met, his upper lip curled up in a snarl and a low growl sounded from deep in his chest. I knew he blamed me for what I did to Alice, so I took his ire while lowering my head.

"Put me down, you jerk." Alice pounded on Samir's back as he lowered her feet to the ground and stepped back. "I can walk on my own, thank you very much."

"And now you don't need to, Human. Stop making things difficult. There are urgent matters at hand."

"Argh!" Alice turned to me. "Can I punch him in the nose, Brooklyn? You are stronger than him, right?"

"You can," Dominic answered with a lopsided smile that made my heart skip a beat. "I can do it for you if you like, Alice."

"There is more than one," Chester let out, still pressed to the glass.

"Intruders?" Samir forgot to reply with something arrogant and annoying and rushed to where we were clustered by the window. "I could use a little exercise."

"Yeah, you could." Alice shouldered her way between

him and Dominic so she could see as well. "You have a muffin top, old man."

"I do not!" The ancient Atua gasped in outrage, staring down at my human friend in horror.

"It's going to be a long night." Groaning, I turned and tucked my face into Dominic's chest.

His soft chuckle vibrated from his chest into my brain, and it made me smile.

Chapter Fifteen

DOMINIC

"I think we should go alone," Brooklyn spoke softly from in front of me right before she stuck her head out to see if anyone waited for us around the corner.

We turned the exterior lights off all around the property so none of the sensors would trigger when we stepped out. All of us could see in the dark anyway, and for the most part we kept them on for Alice. The way she was staying right on our heels I was starting to think we might need to reevaluate her needs. She moved stealthily and silently like the rest of us.

"You will have more luck stopping them than I ever would." Steeling my courage, I stepped around Brooklyn and pressed her to the building by placing my chest against her back.

"What are you doing?" she hissed and froze like a marble statue immediately.

Clearing my throat, I refused to look down at her while she craned her neck to glare at me. Instead, I placed my hand around her hip and leaned to the side, pretending I wanted to see as well if anyone was sitting in wait for us on the side of the mansion.

Another presence registered in my periphery a second before a tiny hand gripped my biceps and Alice stuck her head out from behind me, placing me between her and Brooklyn. "Tell her you're flirting," she whispered.

"Alice suggested…" I started but my mate's groan made the words die on my tongue.

"When in the worlds did she have time to suggest anything? She just woke up like two hours ago." Annoyed, she pushed back to dislodge me, and without confirming it was safe, started walking along the side of the building.

I was glad Samir and Rowen took the other side and the two demons decided to scan every place from the rooftop. I would've never heard the end of it if that pompous ass heard this conversation. As second in line, I kept checking behind me to make sure the human was safe. Seeing she held back and could move faster than I turned, I snatched her arm and dragged her between me and my mate. She would be safer there. Plus, while my mate was arming herself to the teeth, I had to make sure the human was dressed and ready to go. She didn't waste the opportunity to teach me how to act like an interested male.

"You will be surprised how much the human can talk," I told Brooklyn.

"I'm not surprised at all. I've known her longer," she replied and hope poked its head up inside me. Maybe I didn't mess up too much this time.

"Hey guys," Alice piped up from between us. "I know I'm invested in this relationship maybe more than the two of you…" Suddenly, her scream pierced the night when a dagger sang through the air, and I shoved her into Brooklyn's back.

The blade sank deep into my forearm, and I ground my teeth hard enough to crack them as I gripped the handle and yanked it out. Without thinking, I flipped it in the air, and after catching it between thumb and forefinger, I tossed it back where it came from. A pained grunt echoed from the tall topiaries.

"We have to move." Brooklyn grabbed Alice by the hand and darted along the wall of the building, keeping low.

"I think I should shift and sort them out on my own," I grumbled but let her lead us to where she thought would be the best place to go.

"Yes, because it proved very wise for any of us to fight against the Syndicate alone," Brooklyn said wryly. "Look where it got us."

"Didn't you suggest that we should've done this alone a minute ago?" Alice snickered when we reached a rather tall live fence cut in the shape of a spiral. It was wide enough to cover all three of us.

"I meant Dominic and me, not you, Alice. That makes us fight together, not on our own. You just healed and need time to get back to normal. You shouldn't be here in the middle of a deadly fight." Gesturing for us to stay low, she rose from her crouch and peeked around the shrubbery. "I can see three Guardians at four o'clock," she added when she got back down.

I nodded.

"This is only deadly for the poor schmucks who got saddled to come here and fight against all the badasses in this house." The human kneeled on the grass and grinned at us. "And, I have this, too. I'm going to rock their world." Giggling, she reached into a pouch that I didn't notice until that moment hanging around her waist and she pulled out a small vial full of some iridescent silvery blue liquid.

"Are those potions?" Brooklyn did a double take and went as far as leaning close and peeking inside the pouch.

I was curious too but didn't want to lose a hand if I attempted to touch the satchel.

"Yeah, Rowen made them for me one day when we were looking for a cure for you." Alice petted the small bag affectionately. "Now that I'm better, I need to get back to my magic lessons. He is willing to teach me."

"I need you to put a cap on that for now, Alice." Brooklyn locked gazes with me. "I will go at them head on if you would like to shift and circle from behind them," she told me. "Alice, you stay here, and if anyone comes that's not one of us, throw the potion at them first, ask questions later. Okay?"

"Got it." Alice gave us a sharp nod. "Imma lob them in the forehead if they get past you."

"Give me a minute and I'll be in position," I told my mate before grabbing the back of her neck and pulling her close to plant a hard kiss on her lips.

Keeping low, I was out of there before Brooklyn had time to try and rip my head off but paused when I heard both of them snickering and my mate's wistful sigh. I had every intention to get Brooklyn somewhere private after we cleaned out our yard from vermin so that I could clearly state my expectations for our relationship.

Which were none really. I was pathetic. Prepared to do anything she wanted and needed, I was not exactly in a position to demand anything, but I was one hundred percent sure Alice would give me pointers. Her advice was strange, but it worked on Brooklyn regardless of her protests. I was pretty certain I was wearing her down. She acted annoyed, but I saw all the shy, secret smiles she was trying to hide from me.

Warmth spread through me that had nothing to do with my shift, and I relinquished control to my animal that stretched to its full length with purpose. The sooner we dealt with the Guardians, the sooner I would be able to set things straight with Brooklyn.

Shouts sounded from the other side of the mansion, my animal's hearing much more acute than mine picking up everything from the battle Samir and Rowen were dealing with. It appeared they had a few more Guardians on that side, so we needed to hurry and dispose of ours so we could go and help.

On a long leap that stretched more than twenty feet, I sank my claws into the trunk of the tall tree and ripping bark along the way managed to climb to the strongest branch that could hold my weight. My paws padded softly over it, careful not to shake out any leaves or crack any small branches. From my perch, I stared intently at the last place we saw the intruders, and after a moment one of them shifted slightly, giving away their position.

Hind legs bunched up; I was ready to pounce on the Guardians when a shadow averted my attention from the roof. When I glanced there, the air froze in my lungs and my upper lip curled in a snarl as my ears were pinned to my skull. More than ten Guardians were fighting the two demons on the roof of the mansion. We had a bigger problem than we anticipated, and I needed to kill those below me so I could go to my mate.

"There," someone hissed from the area where the Guardians were clustered, and I saw them turn my way. "Up in the tree."

With a loud, enraged cry, I threw myself at the closest

Guardian. My body stretched a full ten feet as it sailed through the air, colliding with the Guardian in a loud clash of muscle on muscle. I swiped my left paw and clawed one of them in half, my sharp nails slicing through muscle and bone easily. The Guardian I landed on wiggled under my weight, but I saved him from his misery by ripping his throat out with ease. Two more were left and they circled around me, giving me a wide berth as if that would save them.

"Am I late to the party?" Brooklyn stepped out from around the tall shrub the Guardians used as cover.

My animal stopped the attack and marveled at our mate when he saw her angelic face, but started purring deep in his chest when she gave him a devilish smile with one fang peeking out from under her upper lip and her green eyes alight with excitement. Red strands were floating like tiny flames around her face where her hair had escaped the elastic tie she used to pick it up in a ponytail.

The male on the right turned and jumped at my mate, right hand raised above his head with a short sword clutched in it. I started to move to tear him to ribbons for daring to even look her way when a sharp pain pierced through me, and I swayed sideways before collapsing on my side. Warm blood trickled down my fur and the stars dimmed for a moment until I shook my head and rose to all fours.

Brooklyn was fighting both Guardians, keeping them away from where I was shaking my head to clear it, and I took a second to look down the length of my body to see the cut. The weapon was not there but the cut, which was a long laceration instead of a small deep penetration wound told me the fucker tried to cut me in half with a short sword and had not stabbed me with a dagger.

"You good?" Brooklyn danced away from two swords coming at her from each side and disarmed the Guardian on her left with a perfectly executed round kick. Her foot connected with his head in a sickening crunch after which he dropped his weapons and collapsed on the grass.

My annoyed snarl was her answer.

"Good. Now come bite this vermin. It'll make you feel better." She avoided the footwork and a few jabs he aimed at her upper body and head. "It hurts me to watch how pathetic he is at fighting."

The male attacked her with a war cry, slashing at her with his sword and trying his best to catch her with a punch or a kick. Like water, my mate slipped through his hands, moving gracefully around the clearing as if she were doing a dance for me. I watched, fascinated through the eyes of my animal, both of us mesmerized by her beauty.

Then she stopped suddenly, and with a firm front kick, she pushed him in front of me. That was all I needed to come out of my trance. Opening my jaws as wide as I could, I clamped it around his middle and lifted him in the air. The male screamed a terror-filled, guttural sound that spiked my adrenaline. Pressing as hard as I could, I shook my head forcing the body to wave in the air like a ragdoll in a toddler's hand before chomping with everything in me and ripping him in half. Blood sprayed in an arch, covering both Brooklyn and me. The moment the Guardian was out, she rushed to my side and dropped on her knees in front of me, her hands holding my maw.

"Are you still bleeding?" Her green eyes held mine, and I could see the urgency there.

I shook my head no, too overwhelmed to speak to her telepathically.

"Thank the stars." She pressed her forehead to mine.

I held my breath, me and my animal both too stunned by the display of gentleness to do anything but close our eyes and breathe her in. Even through the coppery stench of blood, her scent was a lure we could never resist.

An explosion rocked the ground beneath us, and both our eyes flew open wide.

"Alice." Brooklyn gasped and jumped to her feet just as we heard our human friend.

"Not so funny now, huh, fuckers?" Alice's menacing laugh faded under the blasting sound of another explosion.

"She's going to bring the house down," Brooklyn hissed and darted toward her friend.

I was right behind her.

Chapter Sixteen

BROOKLYN

Darkness offered good protection; we were not battling supernaturals but that was the hand dealt to us and we made the most of it. The picture of Dominic ripping the Guardian in half played over and over in the back of my mind as I raced to reach the mansion so that I could start climbing the walls. We fell for the oldest trick and rushed outside where they kept us busy and only the two demons were left to fight the dozens of Guardians who managed to climb on the roof.

"I thought we had wards around the property for this reason." I made the comment to no one in particular, but Dominic, who shifted back to his two-legged form, answered anyway.

"We did. We do?" Sounding uncertain, he reached a hand and snaked it around my waist so he could pull me to the side, and I didn't clip the tree which popped up from seemingly out of nowhere in front of me. "Well, we should."

"Thank you."

"This is so adorable," Alice chirped from next to us when we reached the side of the house and squeezed my upper arm with excitement. My face heated up from her comment and I pretended I didn't hear her.

"I think Alice should…" I started but a thin finger stabbed me in the ribs and made me jerk away from my friend.

"If you say Alice should stay hidden in the house, I'm going to lose my shit, Brooklyn." She poked me again with the same finger, so I frowned at her.

"That hurts," I told her through clenched teeth. That finger of hers was like a thin sword stabbing me between the ribs. She successfully managed to shove it between my ribs for more impact.

"You'll hurt more if you try to leave me behind." She held that forefinger between us threateningly. "I don't know if you've noticed Brooklyn, but every time you leave me somewhere, you end up regretting it because I have a talent for getting into trouble. Tilting her head, she smiled innocently, which I didn't buy at all. "Trouble finds me, actually, not the other way around. I shouldn't be left unsupervised."

"She's not wrong," Dominic piped in although no one asked for his input.

"Umm, hey guys." Alice shuffled closer to me and tugged Dominic by his t-shirt to crowd us. "I didn't want to say anything until later but look what I can do now." She lifted her cupped hand between us, and a red glow appeared low at first but was getting brighter with every breath.

Glancing from me to Dominic with wide eyes, she slowly closed her fist, extinguishing the magic.

My heart jumped hard enough to punch me in the throat.

"Don't do that," I hissed at her and snatched her hand, tucking it into my belly. "What is the matter with you? Do you want to die? Or worse to be taken?" My neck hurt from twisting it this way and that to check if anyone had a chance to see us.

"You all have superpowers, Brooklyn." Getting in my face, she sneaked her free hand between us to push her glasses up. "Why is it such a big deal that I can have some too? Maybe it's contagious and I caught it from you guys. Like a virus."

"Did you show anyone else?" Ignoring the ridiculous blubber, I pushed her at Dominic. "You stay with her while I go help the demons. It sounds like Samir and Rowen are already there."

Sounds of shouts and screams echoed in the night from the roof with an occasional body, or a body part raining around us as if falling from the sky. When I saw Dominic's jaw clench and a muscle started jumping on one side, I knew he wouldn't agree easily to my plan. I should've known he would be easier to deal with than Alice. Good thing the damn wolf shifter was left in the house.

"Who should answer first?" Alice twisted her mouth like she tasted something sour. "What? It's rude to talk over people."

"It has never stopped you before." I pointed out.

"Yeah, but that's you. I like irritating you." She grinned humorously at me. More like she bared her teeth ferally. "It makes you show emotions instead of keeping everything inside. Like right now. Look at that glaring face." She was talking to Dominic with that comment who was trying his best not to laugh.

I wanted to punch them both.

"We need to talk so I can explain everything to you later,

Alice. Please, I beg of you, don't show this to anyone else until we do." Holding her owlish gaze, I beseeched her with everything in me. "What you showed us right now is demon magic."

"What?" she squeaked and jumped away from both of us, her hands stretched in front of her as if to ward us off. "Dear Lord in Heaven, please forgive my sins and deliver me from evil. I promise I will pray every day and have faith."

"You are not religious, Human." Dominic had enough of her antics it seemed, so he glowered at her all annoyed.

"Oh yeah, well I wasn't aware demons existed either, and do you know what that means?" Widening her eyes, she wiggled her head strangely at him. "If demons are real, angels are real, and guess what? The One who made them is real too, probably all are pissed off at me for saying He didn't exist."

"Alice," I started, but she shoved a finger in my face to shut me up. Dominic's eyebrows hit his hairline at the audacity, but I was not impressed.

More bodies dropped from the roof, Rowen right behind them. Slowing his fall with magic, he grunted when he hit the ground, and all the air was pushed out of his lungs, the sigils on his skin flickering erratically, and he rolled to stop his fall. We watched him as he jumped to his feet and grinned at us, exposing bloody teeth and lifting his robes in both hands. With a crazed laugh, he then darted toward the front doors to go back up and fight.

The witch seemed to be as insane as the rest of us.

"You know what sucks though?" Alice said after Rowen disappeared around the corner. "All of you knew but no one told me. Great friends I have. Good for you."

"Demons are not what you think." Dominic was

scowling down at her, but I knew he was wasting his breath. She was more stubborn than a mule.

"I don't want to hear it," she hissed at him, and I felt horrible seeing her in so much distress. "If my soul goes to hell, you are coming with me, buddy. I'll make sure of it."

My snort at Dominic's horrified expression earned me a narrowed glance from my friend. Alice started praying again, popping an eye open every third word to check if we were making fun of her. I kept my face straight, so I wouldn't upset her more. We had a lot to talk about, but it had to wait until all the vermin were dead on the roof.

"Stay with her, I'll be back as soon as the Guardians are gone." I muttered to Dominic, who gave me a sharp nod in answer.

"I heard that," Alice called out after me when I started climbing the side of the house, clinging to bricks with the tips of my fingers.

I couldn't help but smile at her spunk. No matter what we were dealing with, she never allowed it to bring her down. Smooth like a piece of paper, she adjusted to whatever life threw at us and moved on. Maybe we could learn something from a human after all, I decided as I reached the roof. Lifting myself up until my arms were straight and my waist was level with the top bricks, I swung my legs and rolled onto the rooftop.

"Lovely of you to join us." Samir grunted at me and punched a Guardian in the face so hard his skull caved in.

Lucky for me, I ended up on the quieter side of the battle where Samir was standing alone picking off stray Guardians who tried to sneak out and attack the others from behind. The two demons and Rowen were standing in a circle, back-to-back, fighting a swarming cloud of Guardians. It was hard to believe so many of them got onto our roof without any alarms going off. We had to remedy that breach when all this was over.

"You're welcome." My mouth twitched at his wide grin, and I joined the fight with vigor.

Two swords crossed a hair in front of my face as soon as I moved, the chill from the steel cooling the tip of my nose. My back was arched as I bent backward to avoid having my face cut off, and I took advantage of it, hoping to disarm my opponents. Throwing my hands back, I performed a backflip, kicking the weapons out of the hands of my attackers. The blades clanged on the roof tiles, the sound loud enough that some of the Guardians from the other side who were fighting the demons and the witch, turned and rushed to help their buddies.

"You know I can make them go away or even fight each other," I begrudgingly offered just as Samir twirled away from a kick aimed at his chest and jabbed his elbow in the Guardian's face.

"Where will the fun be in that?" my elder griped and promptly shoved his fist into the Guardian's chest ripping his heart out. The organ plopped on the roof with a squelching sound when he opened his fingers, and it rolled out of his hand. "I needed this."

"The attack?" I executed a series of kicks and punches before snapping the necks on both Guardians, one after another.

"To kill something." With distaste, he wiped his bloody hand off on his pants. "Anything. Or I might kill that damn feline."

"I don't think killing my mate would solve your problems." Avoiding his knowing, amusement filled glance, I threw myself at the next Guardian.

"I suppose it would not."

I still heard what he mumbled under his breath but chose not to comment on it. Good thing too, because the distraction cost me a dagger to my side, which could've been worse if I wasn't looking at the scum when he stepped out from the shadows| My cry of pain and surprise was echoed by a roar of a panther from the ground where I left Dominic and Alice.

Samir ripped the Guardian's head off clean with his bare hands, but it was too late. I could hear the panther crumbling bricks as he was climbing the side of the house.

So much for keeping Alice safe.

"It was about time he joined us." The ancient Atua smirked at the shifter as soon as his head popped up from the side. "I thought the only thing you're good at now is sniffing after Brooklyn."

I felt the vibration of the roof when the panther jumped next to me, his weight rattling the structure. With his ears pinned back on his head, he bared his sharp teeth as long as my forearm at Samir on a snarl.

"Stop provoking him," I reprimanded Samir, who was smiling from ear to ear like a fool.

"It's so much fun though." He laughed and danced away from the swiping paw, which Dominic aimed at his head.

"Males." I snickered and found the next Guardian to kill.

Chapter Seventeen

ALICE

"There we go." Hands on my hips, I watched the panther scramble up the side of the building, nearly slipping twice when the bricks crumbled under his paws. "You guys will give me a heart attack one of these days. Pfft!"

Wiping at the sweat that beaded on my forehead with my sleeve, I heard Brooklyn's cry of pain. I looked up and down the side of the house. No one was there. Not even bugs could be seen flying around. Which was weird. If nothing else, there were always mosquitos around the property.

"Maybe they are all up on the roof, too, for a free meal. It's a bloodbath, I have no doubt." Shivering from the picture my mind created about the fight, I laughed uneasily. "They left me behind anyway and I could help in a fight. They know it."

Leaning my back against the house, I crossed my arms over my chest and stabbed the toe of my shoe at the patch of grass in front of me, like it was its fault my friends thought I was a weakling. Not that I was sure how I felt about that demonic magic. Not really. Maybe that was why it was all pitch black and freezing cold when I had barely clung to my life. I must've been in hell for refusing to believe there was a God.

In my defense, no one enlightened me, and they all apparently knew that demons were real. Does that mean it's their fault or mine? And no one per se said '*Yo, Alice! Demons are real.*' So, I had every intention to blame it on ignorance. With a nod to myself, I exhaled loudly and squared my shoulders. Instead of going inside and picking my way to the roof, I figured it'd be better if I patrol around the house. In a worst case scenario, I had the red magic. Demonic or not, I was going to use it to save my ass if it came down to it.

"I should've brought the dog with me." Pushing the glasses up my nose with a forefinger, I picked a side and started walking as softly as I could, so I didn't announce myself if there was anyone slinking down around here.

Reaching into my satchel, I gripped one of the boom juices Rowen made for me, and raising my hand to the side, prepped to throw the vial of potion in someone's face if they jumped me.

"Ah!" My scream echoed around the empty space of the yard when something brushed the side of my face.

Flipping around, I lobbed the vial at whatever it was and jumped a foot when it exploded a dozen feet away. Dirt and grass flew up in the air and pelted me everywhere, including my face when gravity took over and they rained down. As soon as it settled, I saw the moth flopping with one wing, limply, as it twirled to the ground and didn't move.

"Watch out world, here comes Alice, the moth killer." I mocked myself and looked around to check if anyone saw me. My heart hurt for the moth but the poor soul was nowhere to be found. Please, Universe, make sure it's okay while I made sure no one would laugh at me for this stunt. Craning my neck, I couldn't see anyone on the roof looking down either, so I figured I was safe from humiliation. I didn't need another strike against me for why I shouldn't get involved when everyone fought. "I'm taking this to my grave. How pathetic and such a waste of potion, Alice. Get a grip, woman! You should've known better than that."

I wondered how hard it was to make the vials as I picked the grass and dirt from my hair and flicked it away from me with disgust. A few more bodies dropped from the roof, and if I was not mistaken, a leg. Just a leg separated from the body. A shudder made me shiver slightly and I looked away.

If anyone told me a year or two ago that I would watch people being murdered and I'd only shiver because I didn't particularly like the sight of blood, I would've laughed in their face.

How things had changed. For the better, of course.

Life would've been boring, otherwise, without all my friends that were more of a family now.

That was why I had to figure out ways to contribute, and having this demon magic might just be it if I could learn to utilize it, only if God forgave me, which if I remembered anything about religion, He should. As long as I felt bad about it. So I thought anyway. I was sure I could make explosives with it just like the witch to help our cause and protect those I care about. I was practically an angel.

Did it cost Rowen a lot to make the potions? Did it drain his energy? Oh! Or maybe it depleted his magic since he was channeling to charge the fluid. I'd have to ask him when I got a chance and start taking notes. I was an entrepreneur; I could totally make that work. Carefully stepping over low plants and wading around rose bushes, I was so deep in thought that I almost missed the shadow that separated itself from the house.

The moment I saw it, I dived for the first largest bush that would cover me, which unfortunately was a rose bush. Thorns dug into my skin, piercing it in many places, but I was more worried about staying alive than bleeding from a few scratches. It was probably too good to be true to hope whoever that was that they didn't see me, especially after the explosion I caused by tossing the potion at the moth.

"Great job, Alice," I muttered under my breath as I crawled my way toward the group of larger topiaries. "You survived Brooklyn who is as badass as they come just so you could be killed because of a moth. Dumbass."

Nose scrunched up because I was pressing my hands to stuff that was squishy and I couldn't see what it was, I kept crawling as fast as I could while straining my ears to hear if I was being followed. My heart was beating so fast there was white noise in my ears, but I had to believe that I would hear it if someone was chasing me. It was either that or I would've started screaming from the top of my lungs for Brooklyn or Dominic.

Now, that would've been lower than pathetic.

Grinding my teeth, I focused on the red glow in my hands. If I could get that going, maybe I could defend myself from whoever was after me. The fighting from the roof was still in full swing with shouts and roars from up there echoing through the night. There was no doubt in my mind that no one would hear me if I called for help. Or I would be dead by the time one of them reached me. My heartbeat spiked up from the fear choking me and it made me lightheaded.

"I just escaped death's shovel, for fuck's sake." Spitting the words out as quietly as I could, I was zooming toward the topiaries on hands and knees like a baby on crack doing my best to ignore all the twigs and rocks digging into my skin through the fabric of my pants. My glasses were sitting on the tip of my nose, but there was no time to push them up, so I prayed that they didn't fall. I was practically blind without them. With all the magic mumbo jumbo, I thought my eyesight would've improved without them, but no. I had red hand sparks which did something, I guess, but I was still half blind the second the damn mason jars were off my face.

As soon as I reached the thick greenery, I'd be able to look around and maybe even throw one or two vials at whoever was there. So, that gave me a much-needed boost to get my butt moving faster. The majority of the intruders were on the roof by the sounds reaching my ears. Because they were dying there en masse, yet the fight kept going. Unless there was a portal made somehow and new ones were coming through it, all the Guardians sent to kill us were rushing to help their friends on top of the mansion.

Unsuccessfully, I might add.

Palms stinging from the scrapes I earned for my genius idea of crawling across the large expanse of the yard, I finally reached the thick of topiaries reaching toward the sky like gnarled fingers. Leave it to Samir to see this and think to himself, you know what? This is stunning.

Our lives were as gloomy as they could get. Why couldn't he put something like doves or dancing fairies there instead so that we could look at pretty things at least. But no, he had to make sure that even the decorations looked like monsters trying to grab the moon and drown us in our misery.

Almost dying made sure that I'd barely moved out of the bed, so I was panting as I leaned back on the thick topiary, hugging it for dear life. Hand shaking, I petted my pants blindly in search of the satchel so I could check how many vials I had left. My fingers rolled over a couple of them, and I knew that I couldn't use them unless my life was in immediate danger. For a second, I thought maybe I could climb the trees that stood silently in the distance and hide there, but I didn't have energy left to make the crazy dash across a football field of open space.

A branch cracking from a heavy weight was too loud in the silence of the night. The Guardians weren't even worried if I could hear them, they were coming for me and they wanted me to know it. I could hear their snickering and chuckles mocking me for running away like a scared little mouse with my heart in my throat. I fisted my hands, determined to push back the fear so that I could think straight and come out of the situation without relying on Dominic or Brooklyn to save me.

"You can do this, Alice," I hissed at myself under my breath.

The scream of a Guardian flying off the roof, and the sickening pump when the body hit the ground, gave me some much-needed courage. I was not Alice the human. I was Alice, friend of Brooklyn, the vampire, as much as she hated me calling her that, and friend of Dominic, the shifter. I was part of the supernatural world and I'd be damned if I allowed anyone to take that away from me. They could laugh and say that I was imagining things and I was living in fairytales, but I knew better. Being in this world was my destiny.

Now was my chance to prove it.

"Hello boys." I stepped out in the open when I heard their footsteps close enough that I had no doubt I would be able to see them even without my glasses. "You looking for me?"

Acting all nonchalant, I folded my hands at the small of my back and cocked a hip as they watched me as if I had lost my mind. In reality, I was doing my best to bring out that red magic in my fingers and hoping they would come a little bit closer so that I could blast them with it. That was my best chance of surviving this encounter.

Another body came flying down from the roof with a loud thud.

Heart racing, I kept flicking my fingers as if somehow they could spark magic at their tips on their own. With my other hand, I reached for the potions Rowen gave me, so that I could have that as a back-up if the demon magic didn't make an appearance.

Three Guardians stared me down, no doubt thinking I had lost my mind and that they had been punished by being left to deal with a human instead of having an honorable fight with those deemed worthy. Hanging around supernatural beings made me realize that they thought we were lesser, but that wasn't true. They had hundreds of years to perfect their lives. We had fifty years if we were lucky.

Me?

I had thirty-five, the way things had been going.

The Guardian right in front of me smiled wide and menacing. I could tell when he was ready to attack. Closing my eyes and praying that it would work, I flung my hands out in front of me and screamed from the top of my lungs.

Magic burst from my palms, exploding him into pieces. It spread like a spiderweb from the dead Guardian into the other two, making them burst and popping them like grapes as well. Blood and body parts rained down on me, like in some horror movie. All I could do was blink and hold my breath until it was over. It lasted but a second, and everything went still.

"Holy shit." I giggled hysterically.

Chapter Eighteen

BROOKLYN

Thrilled from the opportunity to take all of my frustrations out on the scum in the ranks of the Guardians for the syndicate, I moved like water around them, ripping limbs and throats out as if they were made out of paper.

This.

This was what I was born to do.

I was a killer.

The sooner I came to terms with it, the sooner I could accept it and stop fighting my nature.

A scream pierced the night from below, and hearing Alice's voice speared a sharp pain through my chest. I wanted to rush to her to protect her, but there were just so many of them around us that even if I tried, if anyone was going to hurt Alice, I would've been too late to stop it. Taking a page from Alice's book, I started praying to whoever listened to protect her to keep her safe.

We just got her back this couldn't be how we lost her.

Tonight couldn't be the night I would lose a best friend.

The panther plowing through Guardians like they were

nothing craned his head to look at me down the length of his body. Those green eyes were asking me if I wanted to go help my friend. I had no doubt he would do everything in his power to make the way for me. I shook my head no, surprising not just Dominic, but myself as well. Alice had potions the witch had made for her, and she had the demon magic at her disposal. I had to trust that she could take care of herself.

'And what if she can't?' a tiny voice whispered in the back of my mind, but I pushed it away.

A sword flew in my direction, swiping the air right above my head as I ducked, turned and twisted to avoid being cleaved in half. The Guardians were getting more inventive. They were doing combinations of weapons and pure strength, throwing their bodies at us. They were losing regardless of the fact that their numbers were much greater than ours. From the side of my eye, I could see the two demons fighting back-to-back, their style almost like modern dancing, where they lifted and helped each other out, turning the bloodbath around them into a work of art. Both Echo and Chester had big smiles on their faces, although blood was dripping from multiple wounds they had acquired in the last hour or so that we'd been fighting.

It took me a second to realize what was happening when I found Rowan standing to the side, bent over with his hands on his knees, panting, and looking around him while Guardians were throwing themselves at the invisible barrier he erected around himself.

"Why didn't he tell us he can make those bubbles?" I asked Samir, jerking my head in the direction of the witch. "I could use one of those protections."

"The witch is full of surprises." The ancient Atua said just as he grabbed a head of a Guardian with both hands, twisting and pulling until he separated it from the body. He glanced at it in disgust and tossed it away from him.

"Did you hear the scream?" My panted question made Samir stiffen his shoulders just as an explosion rocked the building.

"She will be fine," the ancient Atua said with so much conviction that I had to look at him despite my opponent trying to separate my head from my body with a large sword.

"We should've taken the wolf with us." My offhanded comment only made him angry.

"Yes, well it's too late now for what ifs, Brooklyn." Redoubling his effort, he ripped into the Guardians with vigor. "I doubt that they brought explosives with them. I have to trust she can take care of herself." Flattening his body on the ground, he rolled away to avoid two blades aiming at his middle. He quickly popped up, grabbed each of their arms and tore their appendages off.

Cries of pain echoed across the rooftop, and I had to return Samir's smile as we continued to fight.

Bright light blinded me for a second, and I had to take cover, particularly at the wide portion of the roof. My hiss of pain when the bright light blitz blinded me was answered by Dominic with a feral growl. He jumped on a Guardian and shook his head until he ripped the body apart and took a running start from across the roof to reach me. On a good note, taking a break for a second gave me the opportunity to realize we were almost at the end of our fight. There were a handful of Guardians, and I hoped that maybe one of them was down in the yard tormenting Alice.

My friend was resourceful. She'd figure out a way to keep herself safe until I could get to her.

The second scream that came much later put me more at ease. Normal friends could recognize each other's voices from afar. Sadly, I knew Alice's scream whether it was one of panic or one of anger and triumph. Whatever was happening down in the yard, Alice was coming out on top. The burst of bright red magic that illuminated the night confirmed my suspicions.

"Smart girl." One glance at Samir confirmed he was paying very close attention to my best friend as well. Returning his nod, I joined back in the fray so we could finish this ridiculous fight.

"What was the Council thinking, anyway?" Punching and kicking, I was talking more to myself than anyone else. "They think they can send Guardians and we are just going to tuck tail and run? We should pack some of these body parts and heads in boxes and express mail them to the Council members with a big fat bow."

"I have better use for these body parts." Rowen spoke from next to me, making me jerk away from him. I didn't even hear him coming. The witch was proving to be a good ally. Sneaky as hell, too.

"You didn't develop ghoulish tendencies, did you?" Samir looked at the witch with a grimace.

"What? No." Ruffling through his robes, he pulled out a vial just like the ones he had given Alice. He threw it at the three Guardians left on the roof and they flew off of it along with chunks of the tiles. Rowan gave Samir an apologetic smile, I guess, for destroying his home. Not that anyone would be upset with him.

"Well, that was fun while it lasted." Slapping his hands on his hips, Samir looked around the rooftop, assuring himself there was nobody else left he could fight. "Now if you would excuse me, I need to go and check on the human. It will make me a poor host if I have allowed my guests to be injured while they visit."

"I didn't get any apologies for getting hurt while I'm here." Rowan chirped, which earned him a glare from the ancient Atua.

"That's because no one invited you to stay." Samir sniffed and looked down his nose at the witch. "Do feel free to disappear at any time. No need to bother with goodbyes, I understand."

"I should go check on Alice." I was halfway there as I said it, so I could jump off the roof and go find my friend. I froze when I heard what Samir said next.

"Your friend is the least of your worries." The ancient Atua smirked at my surprised face. "How about I take care of the human and you sort things out with your mate?" He slowly turned his gaze from my face to somewhere behind my shoulder, and I was too afraid to follow the direction of his sight because I knew that Dominic stood there. "I am no expert on mating bonds, but even I can tell you that nothing good comes out of it if you try to ignore it. The Fates made sure, avoiding it is not an option."

I held his gaze for a long moment, and as much as I wanted to argue with him, I saw the sadness there. Mate bonds were not something you came across often in our world. They were sacred and should be respected.

I knew that. And it was not like I was avoiding it. I just needed time.

To come to terms with it maybe.

I had no clue.

But Samir was right. I had heard what he said to my friend before I stupidly left and got myself kidnapped by the demons. And I knew that she meant more to him than what he was ready to admit, even to himself. He would take good care of Alice. I needed to speak to Dominic alone. With that, I slowly turned to face my mate.

The Black Panther stood rigid, watching me warily, as if I was the wild animal on the roof.

"Hey."

I approached him slowly, lifting a hand so I could press it between his eyes.

Pushing his head firmly into my palm, he nudged me to the side, and I had no other option but to plop on the low wall to keep my balance. It was either that or I had no doubt if he pushed a little harder, he would've flung me off of the roof. On a sigh, I pulled him closer and started scratching around his neck and behind his ears. A soft purr came from the center of his chest and elicited a smile from me.

"As much as I hate to admit that Samir is right, we do need to talk." Pressing my forehead to his, I closed my eyes.

The panther growled something low under his breath, and I giggled from the sound. "You sound like a grumpy old man, Dominic."

If I was not mistaken, the chuffing sound coming from the panther was a chuckle. It kept the smile on my face. And while I listened to my friends' allies, or whatever you wanted to call them, one by one abandoned the roof, I kept my eyes closed and just breathed the night in. Although, one might say the stench of blood, sweat and what not was disgusting. It smelt like freedom and victory: one more day to fight another battle, one more opportunity to destroy the Syndicate.

Nothing smelled better than that.

"It's just the two of us," Dominic spoke when the silence stretched too long around us.

I opened my eyes and found myself still pressed forehead to forehead with him, but instead of the panther, the male was kneeling at my feet. My heart picked up the beat when my eyes locked on his with the same depth of emotion I felt was reflected back at me. I could've rejected the bond, but looking at him now, I realized what kind of colossal mistake that would've been.

He was mine.

I was his as well.

As if he could read my mind, he moved closer, closing what little space was left between us. The scent, which was uniquely him, filled my nose and made me lightheaded with need. My body swayed where I sat on the side of the roof, and a muscular arm snaked around my waist, pulling me ever closer like he couldn't get enough.

I didn't fight it. That need wanted me to wrap my arms around him and to claw his skin because no amount of closeness was close enough. I needed to feel his heartbeat, to feel his breath on my skin, his arms around me, caging me, holding me down, keeping me safe.

These thoughts were something that would've pissed me off not that long ago, but whatever it was he was invoking inside of me, it was stronger than my will. Was stronger even than my desire for revenge.

It was pure, undiluted lust.

It took my breath away.

Panic tried to settle in, but I breathed through it, holding Dominic's gaze, which was the only anchor keeping me rooted to reality. I watched him, breathless, as he lifted his hand and grazed the back of his fingers over my cheekbone with a soft, secret smile playing on his lips. I returned the gesture with one of my own, copying his face and rubbing my thumb close to his eye.

"Do you know what you asked me earlier?" He kept his tone low, the baritone vibrating deep in his chest.

"I can't remember my name right now to tell you the truth." I snorted at my pathetic behavior.

"You asked me to trust you," he reminded me.

"Yes, I remember." Taking a deep breath, I turned my head and pressed my face to his chest. It was too raw and intense to look him in the eye. I felt too much. I didn't know what to do with this much emotion.

"I will ask you to return the favor." Dominic pulled away from me so that I must look at him. "Will you trust me, Brooklyn?"

"Yes," I said breathily.

"I am going to kiss you now," he said.

And I didn't fight it. I closed my eyes, and I tilted my face up to give him better access.

Chapter Nineteen

DOMINIC

She looks so small sitting there on the side of the roof, the red hair like flames dancing around her head with the strands kissing her cheeks because they were just like me, awed at her beauty. Watching her face tilted up with lips parted invitingly for me lit a molten fire inside me. Like a feral beast, I wanted to grab her and kiss her senseless, but I had to stop and look at her.

I wanted the picture of her offering her lips to me engraved in my memory for centuries to come. This female. This warrior that was ready to take on the world all on her own, willingly removed her armor for me.

I didn't deserve it, but I'd take it.

I would take anything she gave me and cherish it for the precious gift it was.

Her lashes fluttered gently before her eyelids began to rise, and I understood that that was my queue. Tucking a curled finger under her chin, I lifted her face and pressed my lips to hers. I had kissed Brooklyn a few times, many of which she probably didn't even remember from the blood-lust. But this, this felt like something new.

The tip of my tongue prodded at her mouth, and she parted her lips for me. I was a drowning man, and she was the breath I needed to live. I breathed her in. Her scent, her taste, it overwhelmed me so much that it took away my logic. I was standing on two legs, but I was also a beast, and my animal acted on an ingrained instinct as he joined in my desire for my mate, clawing at my insides to take her.

I needed this female more than I needed my next breath. Spearing my fingers into her hair, I pulled her closer, standing up and lifting her with me so that I could press her body to mine. One arm around her waist helped me maneuver her so that I could pin her on the side of the chimney and plunder her mouth with my tongue, leaving no nook or cranny unexplored.

A soft moan came from Brooklyn, and suddenly, all the weakness and softness were gone. Placing both her arms around my neck, she used me as leverage to bounce off the tiles and wrap her legs around my hips. The movement separated her lips and left us both panting. I could see her need for me, burning bright in her eyes that were focused solely on me. My heart was hammering against my ribs hard enough I thought everyone could hear it. My erection was pressing against the zipper of my jeans, making it painful to move, and I hissed when I shuffled my feet to get a better grip on her ass.

Arching her back, she grabbed a handful of my hair at the back of my skull and yanked me to her, shoving her tongue in my mouth with a desperate passion. Our tongues danced, twisted and moved and my knees almost buckled when she ground her core over my cock.

I pressed her harder into the chimney, grinding on her

as I started pulling her shirt off. In return, she continued kissing me, slightly pulling back so she could nip on my lip or suck on my tongue before continuing to take my breath away.

She was driving me insane.

"Help me take this off, Brooklyn." I growled as I tugged on her shirt.

"Do you really need it off?" she asked me between kisses, and I could feel her lips curl in a smile on my skin.

"I suppose not." Leaning back, I held her at arm's length with one hand pressed on her back, and I took a hold of the collar of her shirt with the other. The look in her eyes when she realized what my intentions were would have made me laugh if the situation were not so dire in our need for one another. But it was too late, the sound of tearing fabric surrounded us as I ripped her top in half.

"Savage." She snickered and kissed all the brain function out of me.

My fingers dug into her ass, and I held her where I needed her, grinding and pressing on her lips that were driving me insane. She gave as good as she got, clawing at my shoulders, pulling on my hair, scratching my back. If I didn't know that she was an Atua as part of her mixed heritage, I would've thought she was a wildcat. Unable to hold myself back any longer, I pushed her legs down and flipped her around.

Pulling her to rest her back on my chest, I started kissing on the side of her neck. Peppering small kisses where her neck and shoulder met, then back at the base of her neck to the other side and up so I could nibble on her ear. I was going to lose my mind. I was going to take her with me. And every sound, moan or sucked in breath told me she was right there with me every step of the way. Fumbling with the button of her pants made me snarl like the beast that I was, losing patience because I wanted her bad enough to have to fight a shift. My animal couldn't understand why I was taking that long when all he wanted was to seal the bond and rut.

I did, too, but I also wanted to enjoy every minute with Brooklyn. She was more to me than a broodmare. I wanted her smiles, her secret looks, and her touches. I also wanted her trust. Simply?

I wanted her.

All of her.

Brooklyn pushed her ass back and that was all it took for me to lose control. Grabbing her waistband with both hands, I pulled and ripped the pants right off of her. Seeing her perky ass covered with the lacy fabric, off came her panties, and spreading her legs wide made me shake with need. Instead of rushing it, I grabbed her ponytail and turned her to the side so that I could plunder her mouth again. My other hand trailed a path from her ribs and down over her stomach until the tips of my fingers dived into the lips of her mound.

"You're soaking wet." My groan earned me a chuckle from her followed by a moan when I separated the drenched lips with my fingers, and I circled the nub. "For me."

"For you," she agreed and pressed her mound into my hand, grinding and searching for friction.

"We should've planned this better," I told her, panting as I yanked on the buttons of my jeans, trying to get them off. "For our first time, we should have a bed and a door to keep everyone away."

"I don't need a bed or a door, Dominic." Flipping around, she took a hold of my face with both hands, and I froze while holding my breath, praying she wasn't going to reject me. "I need you to take those pants off and put your cock inside me."

I flipped her back around and ripped off every piece of fabric I had around my waist and grabbed her hips with both hands. If I expected her to object, I would've been disappointed. She leaned forward, pushed her ass toward me and waited. Flipping her hair so she could look at me over her shoulder was my undoing.

My cock was pointing right where it wanted to go, giving in to the need I could see written all over her face. I pushed forward, slowly entering her needy flesh. We both groaned at the penetration, her channel parting just enough to allow me entrance. Her flesh was quivering and pulsing around my rock-hard cock, making it difficult for me to move. She was so tight; it was almost painful on each slide in and out.

"You feel so good." I grunted, thrusting my pelvis in an out slow enough to make both of us pant with suppressed need.

"You feel good, too." She kept pushing back, pressing her ass against me as much as my grip on her hips will allow it. "Dominic, I need more."

"Me too, Brooklyn. I just want this to last." My honesty earned me one more of those looks over her shoulder.

This one was open, vulnerable, and dared I say full of love. Seeing it formed a fist in my throat that was hard to swallow. My thrusts slowed, my grip softened, and I realized I didn't want to do this like a shifter would. She protested when I stepped back and I pulled my cock out. But it wasn't for too long. Flipping her around, I put us in the same position as we started. I lifted her legs and wrapped them around my waist.

When I entered her this way it felt like the penetration was deeper. As if we were closer. Having her chest pressed to mine made it possible to feel her heartbeat, too. The organ was punching her ribs as hard as mine was kicking in my chest. And like the fool that I was, I couldn't keep my mouth shut.

"You are my everything, Brooklyn," I told her honestly. "Not because of the bond. But because of who you are, because of what you are."

"A monster." She lowered her eyes and tried to push away from me.

"No." Pinning her to the chimney, I waited until she looked at me. "Not a monster. You are the kindest, the bravest, the most beautiful female I have ever seen in my life."

"You need to fuck me, Dominic, not make me cry." She smirked.

"I can fuck you later." Her head jerked up and she glared at me when I said that. "I'm going to make love to you now."

Whatever she was going to say, was left unsaid because it ended on a cry of passion when I started to move. Slowly at first, then speeding up at times; I kept moving in and out of her body, listening to all the little breaths. All the soft cries and moans told me what she liked and what she didn't. I was learning the female became my life as I joined our bodies into one.

I believed it was me that felt the seal of the bond first. Heat formed at the pit of my stomach and started spreading through my torso at an alarming speed. I knew when Brooklyn felt it too because the sounds she was making were louder, her movements frantic. If I thought that she was wet before, she was drenched now. Her passion was soaking both of my thighs, dripping down both my legs as my thrusts became erratic.

"Faster, Dominic." Brooklyn's nails started breaking the skin on my back. She arched her back, digging the heels of her feet into my lower back. "Harder."

"So much for making love," I ground through clenched teeth and turned her around, her back to my front.

"You can try that later, again." She tried to laugh, but it turned into a moan. "I'll let you practice if you keep doing what you're doing."

"I have every intention to keep doing what I'm doing to you, Female." The pumping of my hips positioned her just right. The sounds of slapping flesh echoed around us in the stillness of the night.

"More," my mate demanded, and I gave her what she asked for. The skin on her hips dented from the pressure of my fingers, and I thought for a second that I should be gentler, until she lifted a leg, pressing her foot to the side so she could push harder against me.

My beast roared inside my head in victory, beyond happy that he was ready to seal the bond. The heat that was spreading through my torso extended to all extremities to a point I thought it was going to melt my skin. Sweat dripped from Brooklyn as well. Fascinated, I watched the droplets trickle down her spine, and I wanted to cherish the moment, but my body had other ideas.

My cock kept pumping in and out of her body, pushing us closer and closer to completion. Her cries were becoming faster and louder, her nails glowing at the chimney tiles. I expected to feel the urge to bite her, but it never came. Instead, Brooklyn pushed her ass back hard enough to dislodge me. Then she flipped around and impaled herself on my swollen cock in one smooth move. My cry of pleasure matched hers a moment before she yanked my head to the side and struck like lightning.

Her fangs pierced my skin, and I exploded inside of her with a roar loud enough to be heard all over Chicago. My hips pistoned in and out of her so fast, all I could do was hold onto her and close my eyes. Her scream of pleasure joined mine a second later, and her channel milked my cock for all it was worth. The orgasm lasted forever, at least that was how it felt until the bond settled into place like slapping an elastic band over your wrist.

We both collapsed onto each other, sweaty, panting for breath.

"Remind me again why we waited this long to do this?" Brooklyn gasped and brushed a strand of hair from my forehead.

"Do you really want me to answer that?" I asked and kissed the tip of her nose.

"Nope, I'm good," she chirped.

My chuckle made both of us hiss when her channel pulsed around me because I was still inside her.

Chapter Twenty

BROOKLYN

"You should've seen it, Brooklyn." Alice stood in the middle of the kitchen, waving her hands excitedly while the rest of us stood, watching her with smiles on our faces. Her happiness was contagious, and we could all use some of that right now.

"Like one second, I was so afraid I thought I was going to scratch myself out of my skin so I could get away." Sinking her fingers into the thick of the wolf who was sitting next to her patiently, she shook her head. "I think it was the fear that made that magic so powerful, you know. He was coming at me, and I was sure I was going to die, so I just slammed my hands into his chest. And boom! It flung him all the way to the house." Throwing her head back, she laughed so hard tears were streaming down her face.

"Oh, we heard it," I told my friend." I am grateful that you are well and alive. I would give anything to have seen that."

"The human is all grown up." Dominic smirked when

Alice gaped at him, her jaw hitting her chest. "She doesn't need our protection anymore."

"I would've happily let you deal with it, Dominic. Don't be an ass." Rolling her eyes, Alice pulled the wolf with her so she could come join us at the table.

"The human has been prickly since yesterday. Maybe we should feed her. She might learn manners then." Samir's voice came out muffled since half of his body was inside the fridge where he was searching for ingredients for whatever he was cooking.

"I scratch and bite as well," she told him and stuck her tongue out at his back.

Very slowly, Samir straightened to his full height and turned to face Alice with a look I couldn't decipher. "You'll crawl and beg, too, Human," he promised.

I had a sinking feeling he had no intention of hurting my friend. Not in a way that she would not enjoy it anyway. Watching her face go red confirmed my suspicions that something was going on between them.

"The sexual tension in this house is thick enough to be cut with a knife." Echo leaned toward Chester and whispered conspiratorially. "And they think demons are sinful."

Everybody laughed at that, and the tension that was twisting the muscles between my shoulders eased a little. I felt calmer, but that could have been because the mate bond was in place and feeling Dominic as if he were a part of me made me content. Hopefully, it wouldn't interfere with my reflexes, and I might survive the next encounter with the Syndicate or the Council.

Speaking of which.

"What's the plan now?" I looked at everyone since we were all in the same bag according to the Council.

We disposed of most of the Guardians that attacked us

the night before, but I was pretty sure that a couple of them got away. After all, the Council valued information more than anything these days. They couldn't stay one step ahead if they didn't know what was coming after them.

And I was there at the top of the list.

"Does this happen often?" Echo glanced from me to Dominic. "How often do they come and attack this place?"

"They have never attacked here," I told the demon. "We should've been more careful when I brought you here. I think we were followed."

"That would explain it." Samir never missed an opportunity to look down his nose at any of us. "You're growing complacent, Brooklyn. It can cost us all of our lives."

"Not all of it would be a loss then, would it?" Baring my teeth at him in a resemblance of a smile, I couldn't stop the happiness I felt when he glowered. "Don't worry, Samir will make sure to protect you. No big bad wolf will be coming for that grandma."

"I'm rubbing off on her." Alice leaned across the table to whisper to Echo. "She makes me so proud. You should've seen her before, she had a stick up her ass just like Samir. I think it's an Atua thing." Stretching as far as she could without laying out fully on the table, she lowered her voice even more." They're vampires, but you know, let them call themselves whatever they want." With an exaggerated wink, she slid back into her chair and lifted a finger to her lips.

"Anyway. Where was I?" Smacking Dominic's chest with the back of my hand to stop his chuckling, I stabbed Samir with a pointed look. "You know this is not going to stop. Now that they have attacked this house once, we will have to defend it every night."

"The best way to win with the bully is to change the rules of the game." Rowen didn't even turn from his task of stirring the sauce over the stove. "If we have learned anything so far, it is that the Council is not good at defense. They will stick to the attacks to keep us occupied so we don't go knocking on their door." Finally, he glanced at me. "Let's not be afraid to disappoint them."

"I was thinking the same." And I nearly laughed when the witch looked like he was about to faint from my admission. "I'm not that much of a horrible person, Rowen, am I? I can admit If I'm wrong, or if I agree with something you say."

"It's the sex." Alice whisper-yelled, cupping her mouth as if that would prevent me from hearing it. "I'm pretty sure they had it last night."

When she saw my glare, she offered me a sweet, innocent smile. "I would agree you're not a bad person at all. I mean you're my bestie, so, hello."

From the corner of my eye, I could see that Dominic was biting his lips in a pathetic attempt not to smile. Which obviously made me want to punch him even more. Chester was grinning from ear to ear while giving a thumbs up to my mate, and I was grateful when Echo elbowed him to stop the nonsense.

"What I never had a chance to explain was the reason why I brought Echo and Chester here." Leaning both elbows on the table, I took a deep breath and explained everything the demons told me after they brought me to their home.

A sea of emotions played across the faces of everyone present, including the few growls and whines coming from the wolf who was sprawled across Alice's feet. Anger, I could deal with, and I welcomed it whenever I saw it burning in my friends' eyes. It was the concern that worried me the most. Especially when Samir tried to avoid my gaze.

"Now would be the time to share whatever it is that you know, Samir." Keeping eye contact, I allowed him a little bit of time to collect his thoughts. The battle was evident in his irises, but we did not have the luxury to play a guessing game. He was right in what he said.

The Council was never going to stop coming after us.

"The cages and the creatures were Frederick's pet project." With a sigh, Samir dragged himself to the closest chair and plopped in it unceremoniously. Very uncharacteristic of him. "If Isiah and I asked too many questions, his psychotic tendencies would come out to play. So, we let him be. I needed to keep my head down and not bring too much attention to myself and what I was doing. Isiah had his own reasons for not asking questions, I'm sure of it."

"If you say that you had no idea what was going on under your roof, I will tell you you're a liar." Echo leaned forward, trying to get in his face. Anger twisted her features, turning her attractive face into something out of a nightmare. The demon in her was coming out in full force. "You don't get to live as long as you have if you're not smart, so stop playing dumb."

"I never said I didn't know what he was doing. I heard the whispers, I had my spies." Rubbing his face, Samir looked every bit of the ancient Atua that he was for the first time. "I just had to pick my battle. Was it more important to argue with him and get nowhere, or keep my mouth shut and make sure Brooklyn keeps breathing?"

Clenching his jaw, he squared his shoulders and looked Echo dead in the eye. "If you want me to apologize, I will not. I do not regret keeping my word. I will never regret keeping her alive."

"He's telling the truth." Rowen turned the oven off and pushed the small pot aside. Snatching a towel, he wiped his hands as he shuffled closer to where all of us were clustered at the table. "Samir may have not noticed me, but I watched him. I have seen many times how he brings attention to himself to keep it away from Brooklyn. More often than not provoking Frederick's ire."

"I didn't know." A metal band was squeezing my chest, preventing me from breathing. "If I knew…"

"I didn't do anything for your gratitude, child." His pride returned, and he sat straighter in his chair. "A man is nothing without his word, and my word is my bond."

I could've kept going, poking and prodding to find out more details about the reason he gave his word to either one of my parents, but I chose not to. Our pasts haunt us without poking at them. Nothing comes out of it, so I dropped it.

Here and now was what mattered.

"I don't think we should waste time," Dominic suggested and took a hold of my chair so he could pull me closer toward him. "They will expect us to need a day or two to regroup and come up with a plan. I think we should attack tonight."

"Attack what?" Rowen finished wiping his hands and lobbed the paper towel in the sink. "Their stronghold?"

"No." The more I thought about it the more I agreed with my mate. "We should hit at the cages. I doubt that they had enough time to fix all the damage we did when you got me out. I kept them busy enough with my bloodlust to make sure that they don't have the time to rebuild it. That's where we should hit. That's their weak spot."

"I agree with you." Samir stood up and leaned on the table to bring himself closer to my face and look me in the eyes. "I don't know what we are going to find there, Brooklyn. And I shall hope you will not hold it against me whatever it is. I made a promise that you would live. I never made a promise to be a good and kind male. To keep our word, one must do atrocious things sometimes. I am not proud of it. Any of it. I do not regret it, however. And let us not forget. I am an Atua. I do what my nature demands."

"Yeah, okay, we get it. You're an asshole. We knew this so there's no need for additional demonstrations." Alice grabbed his shoulder and shoved him away from me with surprising ease. "Can you get out of her face now? Dear God, are you all this theatrical, all the time? Everything must have drama and suspense with you guys. We all agree we need to attack tonight. Let's get dressed, and let's go. We can discuss Samir's shortcomings when we come back and there is cheesecake."

"I really like the human." Chester leaned to whisper in Echo's ear.

"Thank you." Alice made a funny face. "I think?"

"Absolutely fascinating." Echo agreed with a nod. "I think I want to get myself one too."

"Brooklyn and I are friends. I'm not her pet." Shoving her chair back with the back of her legs, Alice jumped up. "And just because I'm trying to talk nice to you, it doesn't mean I trust you. I still pray to God that He will shove you back to hell."

"You do?" Genuinely curious, I cocked an eyebrow at Alice.

"Well, not exactly right now." Shuffling her feet awkwardly, she crunched her nose and pushed her glasses up. "I kinda need them around for the magic, you know. It was fun."

"So, what you're saying is you want to use them and then kick them back to hell?" Dominic started laughing.

"Would you look at that, the human has changed. What happened to the nice and kind Alice?"

"We are at war here, Dominic." Frowning at my mate, she slapped both hands on her hips. "What happened to that kind and nice Alice," she mocked him. "She took a vacation, how about that? And while we are at it, are we ready?"

"Ready for what?" But I was already pushing off the table and standing up.

"To kick some ass, what do you mean what?" Alice rubbed her hands excitedly with an evil smile to make the demons step away from her.

I truly believed at that point that we'd created a monster.

She fit right in.

Chapter Twenty-One

BROOKLYN

I should've known that something was off from the start.

It took us exactly two days to come up with a plan that all of us agreed on. It was astonishing how difficult everyone could be in a group of people where everyone was used to being in charge.

Well, not me.

I didn't care if I was in charge or not mostly because I made sure that I always worked by myself.

"Does it feel off to you?" Alice fidgeted next to me, tucking her face in the collar of the jacket she was wearing.

"I have never seen the place so quiet," my mate agreed with her.

Squinting as if that would make things appear better, Dominic ushered us deeper into the shadows until we all but hugged the walls of the building. We watched the area from across the street, all of us tucked into the wrecked structure of an abandoned warehouse, enjoying the smell of mold, decomposing carcasses of dead animals and what unmistakably was the stench of human feces.

"Maybe it's just the smell making me feel antsy," Alice muttered through the fabric of her jacket. "But we can totally make this an endurance exercise. Me, for example? I can hold my breath for like a minute straight. Now you try it, Brooklyn."

Echo stuck her head out from a few feet away to give me a look that said, *What in the worlds is the human doing?*

"She prattles when she's nervous," I told her with a shrug, loud enough so that only she could hear me.

I didn't care if the demons liked it or not. If babbling nonsense made my friend feel less stressed, she could talk all she wanted, and they would listen. Or they could go away. Having my mind taken over by the bloodlust and the fog clouding my head after it, so that Echo could jump me unaware made sure that I set my priorities straight.

Alice was one of my priorities.

The demons were not.

"Should we wait a little longer, or call it a night?" Rowen slinked up next to us from the back of the building silent enough my heart skipped a beat when he spoke. "It looks like no one is here."

"And you know this because you entered the area, searched everywhere and established it has been cleared out?" Watching him steadily over my shoulder, I waited.

"Well, no." The witch frowned at me. "It will be hard to hide the Guardians if the place was still in use. Not even the grass is moving, Brooklyn. There is nothing there."

He lost me when he mentioned the grass because I was already fully focused on the building across the street as well as everything around it. That uneasy feeling gnawed at my stomach, getting stronger the longer I stared.

"You are absolutely right." I muttered, while my gaze

flicked frantically from one object to another. "Not a blade moves."

"I know." He sounded confused that I was repeating his words back. "I already said that. We can spread out and start reconnaissance missions tomorrow to find where they have holed up."

Alice replied to the witch, but I stopped listening to their back and forward. The whole situation was perturbing, but I couldn't put my finger on what exactly was unsettling me so much.

"Do you see it?" I mumbled for Dominic's ears only.

"What are you looking at?" As always, he didn't question me, only needed more detail on how he could assist me better to solve my problem.

"Nothing is moving. Literally." Frowning, I turned slowly to look at my mate.

His profile was so perfect it took my breath away, regardless of what situation we were in. I watched him scan the entire area multiple times and finally he locked gazes with me.

"You are right." A line formed between his brows.

"Look." I pointed at some wrapper a human tossed on the street that was rolling gently over the sidewalk. "There is a breeze between the buildings, but nothing moves there." My finger stabbed the air in the direction of the building.

"It's an illusion." No sooner than Dominic uttered the words, all hell broke loose.

"It's a trap," Echo shouted just as dozens of Guardians dropped in front of us from the roof.

A dozen or so more rounded the side of the building, swords drawn and ready to end our lives. Dominic and I both reached for Alice and tucked her between us in hopes of keeping her safe. Back to back, we faced our opponents and readied ourselves for a fight.

"What is taking Samir so long?" I hissed through clenched teeth just as the first sword swung at my head.

"Let us hope they didn't get to him first." Dominic reached over my head, grabbed the Guardian trying to stab me in the throat, picked him up and threw him at the wall like he weighed nothing. "The male is unbearable when he is being himself. I do not want to try and see how he is if he's wounded. Or the gods forbid, they wrinkled his shirt."

Snorting, I kept fighting, trying my best to keep the Guardians away from Alice. To her credit, she was not cowering behind us. Every chance she got, she reached her hand out and sent a blast of demon magic at our attackers. Each time she dropped one on the ground, she would giggle, pump her fist in the air and shout 'Bingo.'

"Wasn't bingo what old humans play?" Dominic asked at one point.

"I wouldn't know. She is the only human I know," I told him in earnest.

Echo and Chester yet again stood back-to-back, executing perfect fighting styles, combined with the use of their magic, and again, I was left disappointed that I couldn't just stand and watch. Maybe after all this was over, I would ask the female to show me some of the moves. Their technique was immaculate and effective. Piles of bodies grew around them, but the sea of attackers never stopped.

"Brooklyn." Alice's shriek made me duck instinctively and cold sweat trickled down my spine when I felt the blade cut the tip of my ponytail. "Die!" my friend screamed and slammed both of her hands onto the Guardian's chest.

Bright light illuminated the night, giving everyone a

sinister feature from the shadows dancing on their faces as the demon magic wove through the Guardian from the inside out. But Alice was not done. Stepping over the few bodies we collected around us, she started moving into the sea of attackers, pressing her palms at the center of their chests. By the time they realized what was happening, we could see an end to the cluster.

As the group around us thinned, I wish I couldn't see what was behind them. My mouth cried out. I watched as rows and rows of witches lifted their arms and prepared to chant.

"Dominic, let me deal with this, get Alice out of here," I shouted through the screams, hoping beyond hope that he would listen.

"I'm not leaving you alone," my mate snapped. "She's safer here with us."

"Yeah, because you know nobody needs to ask Alice," my friend chirped from right next to me. I didn't even see she was there as I fought my way to her. "Oh look, Alice in person and she can speak for herself. Why thank you, Brooklyn. I am perfectly fine here."

"This is not a time to be difficult, Alice." A fist connected with the side of my face and bright light exploded behind my eyelids. The taste of blood filled my mouth, so I kicked blindly in front of me before spitting at whoever clubbed me in the head. "That hurt."

"There, it's fixed," Alice drawled after she shriveled the Guardian and turned them into a mummy. "I just learned this, it's less messy." She grinned. "Didn't you say they placed the demon magic on the door to keep Rowen out?"

"Who?" I kept fighting, and I couldn't keep up with her train of thought.

"The demons, Brooklyn. Are you paying attention?"

Her eyes widened while she was looking over my shoulder, and I didn't need a warning to know a Guardian was there. Bending forward, I tackled my friend, and both of us rolled over dead bodies to escape the two swords that clang loudly on the concrete where we stood not a second ago.

"Thanks." Alice panted.

"Don't mention it." Jumping to my feet, I offered her a hand and pulled her up. "If you won't let Dominic take you away, can you please hide. I can't fight Alice if I'm worried that you are going to get hurt."

"Or, I can do this." She glared at me stubbornly, and turning her back to me, she lifted both arms. Red light burst from the center of her palms and formed a dome that grew in size and pushed the Guardians away.

My jaw unhinged, and I stared dumbly with my mouth wide open. My friend created a barrier between us and our attackers. The Guardians stabbed at the dome, kicked it, tried to punch through it, but nothing worked. The witches stopped holding hands and gathered in a circle conversing animatedly, wondering, could they break the seal?

"Alice, no." Echo was trying to fight her way to us. "Don't do that, it will kill you."

The panic I saw in her eyes nearly doubled me over. The demon female was horrified, and I looked at Chester, who confirmed that something was terribly wrong. Not wanting to wait and see what happened, especially since Echo said it could kill my friend, I did the only thing I could think of. With all the strength I had in me, I tackled Alice again.

She didn't even scream. The moment I collided with her, her arms dropped down like a string that had been cut off, and she crumpled on the ground, exhausted. Dominic was right there ready to fight so he could keep us safe, and I had time to check her pulse. She was alive. And the fact of hearing her heartbeat made me lightheaded.

"You will be the death of me, Alice," I told her, and she weakly nodded.

"I'm an idiot sometimes," she muttered under her breath.

"We have a bigger problem," Dominic said from above us.

I looked up to see that he was not watching us. The look of fear on his face curdled the blood in my veins. Slowly and fearfully, I followed his line of sight to find Frederick staring right at us with a look of pure hunger on his face. It took me a second to realize that no, he was not looking at us. He was looking at Alice. And when his eyes locked on mine, the sinister smile he offered me made everything abundantly clear. We were not leaving this place tonight. Not if any of them were alive. Because Frederick had no intention of leaving without Alice. We'd dangled a bone in front of a starving dog.

He was going to eat us alive to get to it.

"What have we done?" Hands shaking, I looked up at Dominic. "Dominic, what have we done?"

Numbness spread through me as more and more Guardians and witches started gathering around us. This was it. This was where we died.

"If we give them what they want, we can fight another day."

Through the fog in my mind, I looked around to find the owner of the voice that spoke. I had to blink a few times to understand what my eyes were seeing. Rowen was crouched next to Alice, helping her stand up. My brain couldn't understand what was happening. All I could do was breathe and battle against the white noise in my ears. It sounded like I was standing too close to a moving train, and it was making me dizzy.

Dominic tucked his hands in my armpits and lifted me up. Like a ragdoll, I dangled in front of him until he talked to me, and his warm embrace helped calm me a little and slow down my heartbeat. I didn't care if I died. But I knew that none of my friends would walk out alive.

I couldn't bear seeing my mate die.

Tingles spread through my arms and legs, and I stupidly looked up at Dominic to find him watching me. "What is he doing?" I asked him as the witch started walking away with Alice.

I tried to follow so I could take my friend back, but my legs were too weak and Dominic was holding on too strong. "Are you listening to me?"

"Trust me that this is for the best." He sounded confident, but his hand was shaking when he cupped my face. "We will get her back."

"Who?" Why was nothing making sense to me, and where did Rowen think he was taking my friend?

"Please, Brooklyn, just breathe." A tear rolled from the corner of his right eye. "The most important thing to keeping her alive for now is to keep all of us alive."

I had absolutely no idea what he was talking about. I didn't remember being hit or stabbed that bad that I couldn't logically reason what was happening around me.

Too late, I realized that everyone had stopped fighting, and that Echo and Chester had forcefully planted their bodies against Samir's chest to hold him pinned to the building. Too late, I heard his outraged screams. And the threats he was throwing at Frederick's face.

"I will end everything you hold dear, Frederick," Samir screamed so loud tendons were standing out on his neck.

In slow motion, my head turned so I could see Frederick. And that was when my heart stopped. I watched numbly as Rowen handed my friend to my archenemy and a triumphant smile bloomed on his face.

"I do thank you for the priceless gift, Brooklyn." The scum bowed mockingly to me, snatched my friend, and disappeared in the sea of Guardians surrounding him.

"Alice!" My brain finally caught up with what was happening just as the witches lowered their arms, and I realized that they had been holding me docile. My scream was full of pain and torment. But there was absolutely nothing I could do to stop my friend from being taken.

"We will get her back, Brooklyn." Dominic held me tight and rocked me back-and-forth, repeating the same thing over and over. "We will get her back, I promise."

But he couldn't promise anything. All of them stood there and let my friend be taken but now they were ready to make promises that they couldn't keep. I saw everything clear now. This was a trap because the Council knew we were coming. There was no doubt that I was getting my friend back, but before that I had one thing to do.

I had every intention of finding out who betrayed us and set the whole thing up.

And when I found them.

They would be cursing the day that they were born...

Also By Maya Daniels

vinci-books.com/restingwitch

Forbidden fruit is sweet... until you take a bite.

I was the dud of my coven—until a failed spell blew up the library
and unlocked my magic. In my panic, I tried a simple spell, but
instead, I destroyed ancient texts, wrecked half the building, and
somehow ended up half-naked in the high priest's office. Now, I'm
totally screwed.

Turn the page for a free preview…

Resting Witch Face: Chapter One

Lesson 1: *don't drink and drive.*

No, scratch that. That was for humans. The real lesson was: don't drink and pretend you're something you are not. Like, acting like a badass witch when you have zero magic. Take it from me because it'll destroy your life. Although that was neither here nor there, when it came to me, since I was screwed the day I popped out of my mother's vagina. She died during childbirth, most probably out of disappointment. I kid you not.

I was a dud born in the most powerful bloodline of witches in the world.

How was that for a sap story?

"Hey, buddy," I called out like we're the best of friends. "Get back down here before you hurt yourself and I get blamed for it. What do you say?" The Kishi demon cocked his head and eyed me like I'd lost my mind. Poor schmuck had no idea that ship had sailed years ago.

My foot wobbled in my designer ankle boots when I

took a step forward, and I did an awkward shimmy-wiggle-swan-dive before I regained my balance. It was what happened when you drank one too many Manhattans and answered a call from your coven to deal with a demon selling illegal merchandise.

"Damn you! If I scratch my boots I'm going to skin you alive just to make myself a new pair. I should've just stayed in the damn bar." The racket of a paint can crashing to the floor and rattling around applauded my muttering. It also stabbed my brain, which was pounding like a shifter in heat when a willing body accidentally stumbled in front of his dick. Don't ask me how I know this, because as brutally honest as I am, I'm not going to tell you.

iPhone held in front of me the same way those pompous asses from the Magi Police waved their badges around, I pointed the flashlight right into the creep's eyes. It screeched like a banshee and scattered further into the darkness while I hissed curses at it. Luckily for the demon, none of them would be taking root, because ... no magic, duh.

What took my coven mates so long to get to the warehouse? If this was a party they'd be lining up at the door since yesterday. As I looked around the dirty warehouse and the misty odor of congealed blood and decaying bodies made my stomach roll, I couldn't say I blamed them.

The fact that Kishi demons had an attractive human face on the front and a hyena's face on the back of their skull was the least of my problems. Kishi demons used their human face as well as their smooth, luring voice and other tricks to attract unassuming idiots— which I definitely was not, shut it I'm not!—and then they proceeded to eat them with their deformed jaws. That would've been fine and dandy if they kept it under wraps, but this one also made an entire collection of body parts to sell on the magical black market. Quite a smart trick when the market was scarce, but not such a great idea for this guy, because he was dumb enough to get caught. That was *if* I managed to hold him back until the others got to the warehouse. With all the alcohol in my blood system, I got this like a hot potato in a bare hand.

Witches more than other supernaturals paid good money for body parts like the ones stacked all the way to the ceiling in the large building, although nobody liked to talk about it. It was that pink elephant in the room we all ignored. No delusions clouded my mind that my coven would "confiscate" the evidence in the warehouse without blinking an eye. I was basically standing in the middle of a gold mine.

The pentagram tattoo on the side of my forefinger tingled, an annoying reminder when my body thought I should be using magic, as adrenaline raced through my veins. My meat suit never got the memo we were shooting blanks. We were as impotent as Mike, my coven's administrator, according to Sissily.

"Go away witch, or die," the demon cooed, his alluring voice gliding over my skin like a caress and leaving goosebumps in its wake.

"Aww, you actually think I'm a witch." My eyelashes fluttered in his general direction as I stumbled deeper into the warehouse. "How adorable," I deadpanned, a serious expression on my face that froze him in his tracks.

Silence followed.

"Ah, you are the useless one." His face poked through the shadows before he fully emerged to sneer at me from over ten feet up, crouched like a gargoyle on the rafters. "I've heard of you. Pathetic." He dismissed me, as his full lip curled over a row of flat, white teeth.

I hated sneering. It reminded me too much of the looks on my coven mates every time they stared in my direction.

Shaking my head to regain my focus, I swallowed hard when the alcohol tried to come up. All I had to do was keep the hellspawn from escaping until reinforcements arrived, but he was pushing his luck. Even a dud could do that if said dud was not a little drunk and teetering on six-inch heels. I eyed my precious boots for a split second, considering using them as a weapon and chucking them at his head, but I changed my mind. Like hell I would mess up a good pair of designer boots for a stupid demon.

The choice was taken from me when he decided to try a trick called monkey in a circus and sailed through the air, aiming his body straight at me. My phone jerked to follow the arch of the jump, and I had one second of an "oh shit" moment before our bodies collided. Never mind me, my iPhone flew from my fingers, crashed on the concrete floor with a resounding crack, and I heard my silk shirt rip at the shoulder when we tumbled on the dirty concrete floor. I just bought that phone.

I saw red.

Fingers hooked like claws, I went straight for his eyes when he tried to straddle me. Somewhere in the back of my mind I was aware that if he bit me the poison from his kind would kill me in less than an hour, but I had liquid courage, louder than the alarm bells cheering me on. The demon didn't expect me to claw at his eyes, so when my nails made squelching mush out of his eyeballs, his human face roared at me. If I was in the right mind, I would be shaking in my skin. As things were, he resembled a chihuahua nipping at my ankles to my muddled brain. Wretchedly vile breath melted my makeup and I gagged, barely holding back the bile so I didn't puke all over both of us.

"It's called a toothbrush, asshole." I hacked hard enough to cough out a lung while jamming my forearm in his throat to hold back his snapping jaws. The Kishi demon was trying to munch on my face, for fuck's sake. "You should use it, damn you."

Desperate times called for desperate measures, and, as much as it pained me, I had to sacrifice my boots. My leg swung up like a slingshot, caught him on the side of the head, and he went down hard. His head bounced off the concrete, and his skull cracked with enough strength to be heard over the heartbeat in my ears. The air whooshing out of him satisfied my need to hurt him like he hurt my poor blouse. It was also new and cost me an arm and a leg. Using the time I had, I scrambled on my knees, yanked my poor boot off, and nailed him in the neck with the heel. The demon gasped, probably still dazed from the kick, but apart from a few spastic jerks, he didn't attempt to flee. Or move again at all, but that would be semantics.

They might think that was how I found him.

Right.

With a sigh, I dropped on my haunches not a moment too soon before the solid thump of feet came from the entrance behind me. Light jiggled up and down over the stacked shelving from the flashlight the person held, and I looked down my shoulder at the flipping piece of silk that used to be a soft olive color. Dirt, sweat, and dried blood from the scrapes on my upper arm turned the silk some disgusting color of brown. I frowned at the flapping fabric.

"Hands up where I can see them," the owner of the flashlight barked from behind me.

Great. Instead of my coven mates, I had to deal with a human cop. Just my luck for the night, it seemed.

"Do I look dangerous to you?" My head twisted so I

could squint at him over my shoulder, and a bright light stabbed me in the brain like a pickaxe. "Are you trying to blind me on purpose, or is this how you pick up chicks all the time? If they have a flashlight burning their retinas they can't see your ugly face, huh?" Oh yeah, I recognized the voice better than I should've.

"Hazel? What in God's name are you doing here?"

"Getting a tan. You?" I chirped brightly and regretted it when acid filled my mouth. I would never drink again.

"Don't be a smartass. I'm seriously asking what—" His words stopped when he noticed my ripped shirt and one bare foot, and he shuffled closer. I was pretty sure having my skirt bunched up around my hips and flashing the creases of my ass didn't help, either. Goddess, I looked a mess.

"Are you hurt?" His hulking frame kept moving closer, sending my heart to gallop in my chest.

"No, wait." My sudden shout stopped him in his tracks. "Stay there, Davon, you don't want to get bitten." Think Hazel, think.

"Bitten? What the hell, Hazel. Get away from there right now. What's in there?" When a gun cocked, I knew the jig was up. If he saw the demon, there was no doubt in my mind I'd be in more trouble than I already was.

"It's a dog, okay. Stay back because if you spook it, it'll bite me. Then I'll be pissed. Do you want that?" Where the hell was my coven?

"What kind of a dog?" Tone dripping with suspicion, his feet scraped the floor as he cautiously moved closer again. If he saw the Kishi starfishing it, not even my grandmother could cover the mess up.

"You are the one with a flashlight, Davon, so why don't you tell me. I'm not playing games when I tell you to stay back. Look at my face." I added an additional scowl for good measure, shuffling on my knees to hide the Kishi sprawled a couple of feet away, deep enough in the shadows not to be visible for the moment.

"What about it?" I could've laughed at the weariness in that loaded question, but he did stop coming closer.

"Does it say approachable to you right now?"

"It never does," he muttered, and I grinned at him like a fiend. "This is crazy. You don't get to boss me around after you dumped me."

"I already parted with my right boot, and I love these boots. You wanna try the left one? I can nail you in the fore-head or in the jingleberries. Your choice," I threatened while internally freaking out. Being a bitch to Davon wouldn't work much longer. It never did. He would do the opposite of what I told him just to spite me. I could feel it.

"Hello," a female voice called from the entrance of the warehouse, and I deflated like a balloon recognizing my best friend Sissily. About freaking time. The demon was dazed, but he wouldn't stay down much longer. And if he woke up with Davon here, I had a nagging feeling my body parts would join those scattered around the warehouse in jars. Courtesy of my grandmother, of course. The demon didn't have shit on her when that witch got pissed.

"Stop right there. Police." Davon pointed his gun and flashlight at Sissily's face. Protecting her poor eyesight with a forearm flung in front of her, she blinked at him as if ready to say something.

"Is this your dog?" I rushed to say before she screwed me over. You never knew what would come out of her mouth. "It might be injured, it almost bit me."

"Hazel ..." Davon started in a warning tone.

"Yeah, oh thank goodness you found him," Sissily

gushed, overdoing it a little, if you asked me. Whatever Davon wanted to say was silenced, thank the goddess.

"If this is your dog, Ma'am, I must report it, I'm afraid. It attacked a civilian, and it's considered dangerous." Davon, the good cop he always was, started reading Sissily her rights while she rolled her eyes.

I sighed, pinching the bridge of my nose.

"Oh, shut up human." Her hand flicked when she had enough of his word vomit, and she zapped him hard enough the poor guy convulsed a long moment before he passed out, the gun and flashlight clattering on the concrete.

Then she turned her blue peepers my way and gave me a once-over. Although her blonde hair was smooth and all in one place, and her pencil suit was sharp enough to cut a finger off, Sissily had no right to grimace at me. Someone should tell her "I bit a rotten lemon" was never a good look on a chick. Just saying.

"If you say a word Im'ma boob punch you." Pushing off the ground, I swayed, and for the second time I failed to glue the ripped silk sleeve together. "Are you alone?" It was improbable, but a girl could hope.

"The others are not far behind me. I had a feeling you'd jump right into this, so I made sure I came before anyone else. What do we have?" She sashayed closer, giving Davon a disgusted look.

"Kishi demon." I glared at the asshole who finally stirred with a groan.

"How do you find yourself in these situations, Hazel?" Ignoring her, I was still messing with the sleeve, so with a sigh, she took her jacket off and handed it to me.

"Thanks." Limping a couple of steps forward, I plucked it from her fingers. "And I wasn't kidding about the boob punch. I'll even twist your nipple until you scream if you don't keep your voice down."

"You do know we're not five anymore, right?"

"What's your point?"

I could tell she had so much to say just by the tightening of the tendons on her neck. Her throat worked, her mouth opening and closing until she gave up and shook her head.

Yeah, exactly my sentiments.

"Where's your other boot?" She followed the elaborate swirl of my finger until it pointed at the demon. My beautiful, precious boot was sticking out of his throat, covered in black blood and gore. Then she arched an eyebrow, which should've looked stupid on anyone except me, but on Sissily everything looked good. If she wasn't my best friend and if I had magic, I would've hexed her with warts. I hoped the girl knew how lucky she was that I loved her like a sister. What surprised me more was she loved me back the same, even though I was an asshole. At least most of the time.

"I've always told you fashion is a weapon if you learn how to use it. Did you believe me? Of course you didn't." My smirk earned me a twitch of her mouth. If anyone knew Sissily they'd know it for the huge win that was. She never smiled on a job.

"Danika is going to lose her shit." We both shivered at that.

As if saying the name conjured her, my grandmother's power preceded her presence, filling the warehouse with magic and saturating the air with the strong scent of ozone.

"Hazel Byrne." I flinched when my name echoed in the silent building, and Sissily copied me sympathetically. "Show your face this instant." My grandmother swooped in like a hungry vulture honing-in on a roadkill.

Me. I was the roadkill.

Thankfully, the lights came on inside the building, blinding me momentarily as thumps of many feet scattered throughout the warehouse. Our coven mates spread around the vast space like ants. I blinked like an idiot a few times until my vision cleared, and that was when I saw the look on her face. Cold, emerald eyes sharp enough to cut a diamond rolled over me from head to toe, assessing and judging while telling me she found me lacking in many ways. I gulped and tugged Sissily's jacket closer. Then Danika's unreadable gaze fell on Davon, who took a lesson from the Kishi demon and was starfishing it in the middle of the damn place. She stilled at the sight of a human cop and stabbed me with a glare afterwards.

"That was Sissily, not me." The words burst from me so fast I almost spit on my lower lip.

"Snitch," my best friend hissed, but her chin jutted out and she stepped closer to me.

"Every bitch for herself, remember?" I mumbled behind my hand when I raised it to wipe my mouth in case I was still drooling. Those Manhattans were buzzing in my head like a cloud of bees and making my tongue too thick for my mouth while I swayed where I stood. Oh boy was I screwed.

Sissily snorted but coughed to cover it up. Her reaction earned me a disapproving look from my grandmother, which I felt all the way to my soul. The woman saw everything no matter how hard I tried to hide it, and her hearing was better than a vampire's. I didn't have to guess because I *knew* she heard us.

I was the best fighter they had in our coven. Hand-to-hand or weapon combat, I could take them all down, and that included our high priest. But thanks to my lack of magic, I somehow always ended up looked down on, especially by Danika Byrne. Even when I did get the job done.

One demon stabbed in the throat with a designer boot, case and point.

"We will speak back at the coven." With flare, she spun on her heel, her long dress billowing behind her as she stormed out of the warehouse and left me grinding my teeth.

"Let's go." Linking her hand through mine, Sissily tugged me along with her because she probably assumed I would run. And honestly, I thought about it for like two point five seconds. It was pointless since everything I had was in the house I shared with my grandmother, but it sure was tempting. I wobble-limped alongside Sissily, glancing at my coven mates as they packed everything, including the Kishi demon I apprehended.

"She will chill out by the time we get back." My best friend gnawed on her lower lip, not believing her own assurances.

"I don't care." My shrug didn't fool her since I was patting my hair to smooth it and probably looked constipated just thinking about facing my grandmother behind closed doors.

Because Danika Byrnes never chilled. Like ever. My grandmother was born with a stick so far up her ass the goddess herself couldn't find it if she tried.

She was going to hand my ass to me, and I had no other choice but to take whatever she dished out. A sinking suspicion that it would involve cleaning churned in my stomach right beside the booze.

There was a first time for everything, though. She might've grown a heart in the last twelve hours. Or took it from some random jar and shoved it in her chest. My head tilted to the side, I contemplated it for a second.

One look at my grandmother's disappearing form, with

those stiff shoulders and that head held high, killed that hope. There was no escaping a punishment.

With a groan, I followed my best friend into the belly of the beast.

The whole way back to the coven, I kept trying to picture my eyeballs floating in a jar on top of my grand-mother's desk.

They were a nice shade of golden honey, if I did say so myself. I'd have them in a jar too if I didn't need them.

Resting Witch Face: Chapter Two

The Gatekeeper's coven was located dab smack in the middle of Cleveland, of all places. The temple walls stretched high toward the sky like the open mouths of baby birds waiting for a worm to fall into their gaping maws. A domed ceiling made of glass, to better see the full moon each month, covered almost half the block. Made out of black stone, the building looked menacing, and the three keys – a symbol representing Hecate- painted in blood red above the tall double doors of the entrance stood out stark against it. Since it was late at night, magical flames were shooting seven feet tall on each side of the stars leading to it, casting it in an eerie-hellish hue. No wonder humans gave us a wide berth.

Pausing at the bottom of the marble steps that would lead me inside, I glanced up and down the street. An urge to book it down the sidewalk and find a place to hide for a day or two was very tempting. However, with only one boot and still mostly drunk, there was no way I could outrun Sissily.

She might sympathize with me, but she was a stickler for the rules, and she was smart enough not to want to anger Danika, unlike me. I had no doubt she'd tackle me and drag me kicking and screaming inside by the hair. She did that once in middle school when I didn't want to go back inside with her after lunch break. The humans mulling around would be no help, either. Ever since we came out of the closet, so to speak, they gawked like we were circus freaks but wouldn't come closer than a few feet, as if magic was contagious and they might get infected. I wish it was.

There were exceptions like Davon the cop, but those were few and far between. We were "the others," and unless they needed help, humans wanted nothing to do with us. At least there were no pitchforks or burnings at the stake involved, so not bad I guessed. That was why my coven was very strict. The government told us we were all good to live among humans as long as no problems came up by *any* supernatural being, not just us. So, the high priest and my grandmother—to be honest it was probably all her because the priest was practically a mute when around her—decided we would boss the supernatural world around. The magi police force was just a front for posturing. We were the ones that got down and dirty. And destroyed perfectly new pairs of designer boots in the process, I'd like to add.

Sissily took my elbow and waddled me up the steps when I took too long to move. Chewing on the inside of my mouth, I allowed my fear to choke me until I reached the double doors, and then I squared my shoulders. Whatever issues I had would be left at the door. No one needed to know my shit. It was none of their business, anyway.

The inside of the building was also painted black, with a hallway like one long intestine twisting around offices, ritual rooms, guest reception halls, and the library, of course. Our pride and joy, with knowledge gathered for generation after generation by magical families. It was the largest collection in the world, and the love of my grandmother's life. I personally used it to hide from idiots when they got annoying, or to pretend I was busy when we had a ritual scheduled. If I was busy, I couldn't participate and see all the pitying looks or sneers thrown my way.

"You ready?" Sissily mumbled under her breath and dragged me out of my spinning thoughts.

"No."

"Hazel."

"Why does everyone think saying my name will help anything?" I jerked my elbow out of her pinching hold and tugged hard on the borrowed jacket to straighten it. My balance went sideways, and I pitched forward, but she tugged me back before I face planted. "Let me tell you, it does nothing but piss me off and feed my anxiety. I know what my name is. I've had it my whole life, thank you very much."

"You're stalling."

"No." I gasped dramatically. "What in the world gave you that idea?" Sissily rolled her blue peepers at me. "I really don't want to go in. I might puke all over her desk."

"You're so stupid." She snickered and bumped my shoulder. For her sake, my lips pulled to the side in a pathetic attempt at a smile.

With a sigh, I continued my impersonation of Quasimodo hobbling down the hall on one high-heeled boot and one bare foot, darting glances at the candelabras lining the walls. Black pillar candles burned in clusters with blue flames, the magical fire standing straight without a crackle or a flicker. They always looked like a painting that gave off light to me, and it didn't matter how many times I saw them.

"They are expecting you." We hadn't fully rounded the corner yet, but Mike made sure to shout it like he was playing bingo and just won. He leered at Sissily, but as soon as he met my glare, his head ducked down so fast he almost headbutted the desk.

"I see you didn't take your meds today, Mike?" I jabbed him conversationally, and Sissily snorted.

"What? Yes, I did." His face snapped up and reddened like a tomato. "Hey, I don't take medication."

I pursed my lips, eyeing him and pretending like I didn't believe him.

Something told me if I kept looking at him his head might explode. I was willing to test that theory, but I felt Danika's magic reaching, plus Sissily nudged me to get moving.

"Maybe you should." My suggestion to the creep in passing left him sneering. "Meds won't grow your brain, but it'll help with your complexion."

We left him stuttering and talking to himself about bitches and the goddess knew what other fairy tales he told himself. After he dared to treat my best friend like she was his personal punching bag while she dated him, I made it my business to mess him up every chance I had. I was pretty sure he cast a protection spell around himself specifically against me so I couldn't physically harm him. Good thing, too, because I didn't trust myself not to fillet him like a fish.

I flung the door open without a knock and hobble-hopped inside my grandmother's office with Sissily nipping on my heels. Stopping in my tracks, I took in the large, ornate-oak desk Danika Byrne sat ramrod straight behind. High Priest Shadowblood was behind her right shoulder, his face pinched so tight it looked like he was trying not to fart. His slicked dark hair, long, thin nose, and pointed chin brought the image of a crow perched on my grandmother's shoulder to my mind every time he did that, although I never dared mention it. But it wasn't those two that made me freeze with one foot in the air and one hand gripping the doorknob.

No, it was the third person in the room just to the left of Danika. In his late twenties to mid-thirties, he was a face I'd never seen before between these walls. His blond hair was shaved close to his skull on the sides, with the top left longer to drape over his forehead in a wave. Eyes the color of melted chocolate flicked my way when I opened the door, and they widened in interest—not enough to be obvious, but since I was staring at him like an idiot, I noticed. A square jaw and a nose with a slight bump at the bridge like it had been broken a time or two framed full lips more suitable to a woman than someone like him. Wide shoulders stretched his indigo button-down shirt, which was tucked into the waistband of dark slacks that emphasized his narrow waist and muscular body. I gawked for less than five seconds, but it was enough for one corner of his mouth to twitch. That little quirk snapped me out of my daze.

Spinning around, I bolted out of the office and plowed Sissily down. She would've fallen on her ass if I didn't catch her by the arm and drag her back out with me. The door closed behind us with a loud thump when I bodily carried her to the desk where Mike was still muttering curses at me.

"Give me your shoes." My best friend squeaked when I plopped her ass on the desk.

"What? Why?"

"Shoes woman. Now." My hand was wiggling in her face to show my urgency. "Questions later."

I yanked them off her feet myself because I had no time to explain why having shoes instead of one boot—regardless of how pretty said boot may look—was so important. Lifting her leg up pushed Sissily until she was leaning on her hands, and if I wasn't in a hurry I would've chortled at Mike's face. Poor schmuck almost swallowed his tongue when he received a face full of a ponytail, and his saucer-like eyes told me he didn't miss Sissily's boobs sticking up from her arched back. I even stabbed her foot in my one boot because I was a good friend like that, and then I was yanking her along with me to enter the office for the second time. She'd probably replace my shampoo with glue to pay me back for this, but I'd deal with it later.

When I stepped back inside the office, my grandmother arched an eyebrow not looking very pleased, which I ignored, of course. Being the nice little witch I was, I waited for Sissily to limp inside before I closed the door and guided her to the closest chair. Her blue eyes were spitting daggers at me the whole time. As Sissily dropped on the uncomfortable chair, I went as far as petting her head like a puppy that did potty, ignoring her glare the entire time. Then, I turned and beamed at everyone in the room, giving my grandmother a pointed look towards blondie that said help a girl out but I had a feeling my plea fell on deaf ears.

"Hazel, what happened tonight?" Danika Byrne got down to business, stapling her fingers under her chin and leaning her forearms heavily on the desk. If looks could kill, Sissily would be reading my obituary right now.

Smile frozen on my face to flash my pearly whites, I

widened my eyes at her. "What?" My lips didn't move as I pushed the question through my teeth. My best friend groaned from the side.

"What in the goddess's name is wrong with you?" I swore lightning flashed in Danika's emerald eyes. "Are you hurt? Did the demon do anything to you?"

"We don't discuss coven business in front of strangers, Dani—I mean, Ma'am. Grandmother," I added that last bit lamely as an afterthought, and the thunderous expression twisting her features told me she didn't miss it.

"River Blackman is an apprentice of our high priest, Hazel." She looked down her nose at me like I was supposed to be psychic and guess who was who around here without introduction. "There are no strangers."

Wait, what?

"You can have your shoes back." With a groan, I turned to Sissily and started tugging the shoes off my feet. I shoved them in her face, and she recoiled as if I'd thrown snakes at her.

"I don't want them." She attempted to slap my hands away with a mortified look on her face, but I was very persistent when I needed to be.

"Well, you're having them." I jabbed them at her again. "Give me my boot."

"What in the world is going on?" We all ignored the high priest when he mumbled at no one in particular, sounding perplexed.

"You are aware that you are nuts, right?" Sissily muttered under her breath, but she tugged her shoes on, and I yanked the one boot over my foot.

"Of course. I'm an asshole, Sissily, but I'm not stupid." She blinked at my incredulous tone, but I was already turning toward the rest of the people in the room.

A muscle twitched under my grandmother's eye.

"When the call came for the demon, everyone that answered was at least twenty minutes away. Everyone in this room knows they are sneaky and fast." I figured I'd get it over with. "I was closest to the demon, so I answered the call and made sure he didn't escape. Long story short, he is in our hands and the warehouse ransacked ..." Danika's scowl was a creature all on its own. "I'm sure you don't want to hear my internal debate about sacrificing my new boots so he didn't get away, Grandmother."

Grating on my nerves was the fact that River's eyes were dancing with suppressed humor. *Laugh it up, asshole, because I'll make you cry soon enough.* I wasn't sure he read the message I shot his way through my narrowed gaze, but he couldn't say he wasn't warned. Being a dud was a sure thing to get you bullied in a coven full of powerful witches, so instead of dealing with that, I became a master at cracking their noses with my fist. The blondie wouldn't know what hit him.

"I do want to hear every detail there is. Starting with what possessed you to go there in the first place. Fighting a demon without magic is unacceptable." If she noticed my flinch, she didn't show it. "He could've killed the last of the Byrne line, you insolent girl."

"How's this for a recap, Danika?" I snarled. The gasp from Shadowblood sounded scandalized when I slapped both hands on her desk and leaned forward so we were at eye level. "I can kick any demon's ass, including every idiot you have inside this coven, in six-inch heels, without breaking a sweat, and with my arms tied behind my back. I showed up at the warehouse, cracked the demon's head on the concrete like a melon, then I stabbed him with my new boot. Which you owe me a new pair, plus an iPhone, just so you know. Then the rest of you waltzed into posture with your magic and clean up the place. That good enough of an explanation for you?"

"How dare you speak like that?" High Priest Shadowblood stuttered, his neck elongating as he tucked his chin in. "You are not a savage, young lady."

"Aren't I, though?"

"Show respect to your grandmother," he snapped.

"You got one thing right, pops." My empty stare flicked his way, and he took an involuntary step back. If they don't string me from the roof tonight, I'm honestly never drinking again. "*My* grandmother, and I'm doing exactly what she taught me. To quote her, 'you treat people the way they treat you.' So, I will talk to her however damn well I please. In this case, I'm showing her the same respect she gave me." I believe Shadowblood was about to have an aneurism.

"Hazel," Danika leaned back in her chair on a sigh, all fight draining out of her. "I wasn't trying to insult you because you have no magic."

For an old witch, barely any lines were visible on her beautiful face. She might be a stick-up-the-ass nag, but no one could dispute the fact she still turned heads. Midnight blue hair spilled around her face like a waterfall, bringing attention to her alabaster skin and piercing emerald eyes. Tall for a woman, she was curvy where it counted, but most admirable of all was her presence. When Danika Byrne walked into a room, you knew it even if your back was turned.

"No, you were complimenting me on a job well done." With one last stare at Shadowblood, I pushed off the desk. "If we are done here, I need a shower. I can smell the Kishi demon on my skin."

"I need you to promise me—"

"I will not step foot anywhere where your precious

witches with magic need to go." My smile could cut glass when I looked at her over my shoulder. "I'll just stand back and look pretty."

"You are not replaceable, Miss Byrne—" Shadowblood started, but I cut him off.

"No, I'm to be kept as a broodmare, High Priest Shadowblood. I'm aware." That got the reaction I expected from my grandmother.

"For the next week, you will be cleaning the library, Hazel," Danika snapped and stood to her full height, which was a couple of inches higher than mine. She did it on purpose so I had to look up at her. *Nice power play, Grandma.* "And the ritual room, too, until I say that you are done. Am I clear?"

"Crystal." I dared a glance at River, but with his hands clasped at the small of his back, he was frowning at his boots. *Welcome to the Gatekeeper's Coven, blondie, this is how we treat family.* The guy hasn't done anything to me, but just seeing him standing behind that desk with Danika and Shadowblood put him in my shit bucket, too.

"Let's go," I called out to my best friend, who was in the office for moral support more than anything else.

We almost made it out the door. Almost.

"Sissily, you'll join Hazel in her tasks." My grandmother was already back in her chair and had turned to say something to River Blackman, a blunt dismissal of us if ever I saw one.

We spilled out of the office without another word. "Why do I pay every time you get into trouble, little jerk?"

"Because you are the only one that can call me that and live, big jerk." I threaded my arm through hers, leaning against her for support.

"True." She sighed and placed her head on my shoulder. "On a good note, not even you can get in trouble inside a library."

Lesson 2: *never tempt fate.*

That bitch bit.

Grab your copy…
vinci-books.com/restingwitch

About the Author

Maya Daniels, USA Today Bestselling and multi-award-winning supernatural suspense author, is a fun-loving woman with many talents.

She traveled the world, gaining life experiences that helped her career as an investigative journalist, as well as her storytelling. Maya writes compelling tales of magic, mythical creatures, loyalty, and life-changing friendships with snarky female characters—much like herself.

Her travels have taken her to Europe, Africa, Asia, Australia, and America. Born with her feet in motion, she currently resides in Ohio, spinning her next epic story that you will not want to put down.

Her biggest 'sins' are her love of chocolate and coffee—through an IV drip! One to never sit still, Maya practices Reiki healing, different types of martial arts, reads about the arcane, talks to furry creatures more than humans, picks up a sledgehammer for home improvement, and travels with her fated mate, seeking her own adventures.